THE GUNSMITH

#22

BULLETS AND BALLOTS

THE GUNSMITH

#22

BULLETS AND BALLOTS

J.R. ROBERTS

SPEAKING VOLUMES, LLC
NAPLES, FLORIDA
2013

THE GUNSMITH
#22 BULLETS AND BALLOTS

ISBN 978-1-61232-625-2

To a couple of loyal Gunsmith readers,
Michael Madonna and Robert B. Rice, Sr.

Chapter One

The girl was having definite problems, but not as many as the man underneath the buckboard. From his position on the rise above them Clint Adams could plainly see what the trouble was and what had probably caused it.

Apparently the couple had been traveling in the buckboard in a great hurry and had struck one of a few large rocks that were scattered about, upsetting the wagon. The girl must have been pitched free, but the man had been caught underneath when the buckboard flipped. The girl was now trying vainly to raise it off the man with her bare hands.

"Let's go, Duke," Clint said and kicked his heels lightly into the big gelding's flanks.

As they approached the pair the girl turned her head toward them. She was both young and pretty, although looking, understandably, very distressed at the moment.

"Looks like you could use some help," Clint said, dismounting.

"We'd be very grateful, mister," the girl said.

The man appeared to be much older than the girl, possibly her father.

Clint approached the buckboard and examined the extent of the man's predicament. From what the Gunsmith could see, the man's legs weren't crushed, but merely pinned underneath.

1

''Could we lift it together, mister?'' the girl asked.

''We might be able to,'' he said, ''but there's no point in trying when we have an easier way right at hand.''

''What way?''

''That tree''—Clint pointed to a nearby tree with a large branch that was almost hanging over them—''and my horse.''

''What—?''

''Just wait and watch,'' Clint said.

He walked to Duke and removed his rope from the saddle. Trying not to increase the pressure on the man's legs, he secured one end of the rope to the axle of the overturned buckboard, tossed the other end up and over the large branch, and then tied it off to the pommel of his saddle.

''Okay, big boy, let's back up and keep the tension on that rope,'' Clint said. ''We don't want to bounce that buckboard on the man.''

Very deliberately, Duke began to back up, taking one step at a time, and when the buckboard had been lifted the girl helped the injured man crawl out from underneath it, and Clint had Duke lower the buckboard the same way, one step at a time.

When Clint reached the pair the girl was asking, ''Are you all right, Pa?''

''I'm fine, girl,'' he replied, sounding annoyed. ''Don't be making such a fuss.''

''Better let me check those legs, mister,'' Clint said, but as he bent over to do so, the older man reacted violently.

''Don't touch my legs!'' he shrieked, and Clint withdrew his hands as quickly as if he had scalded them on a hot stove.

''I was only trying to help,'' he said.

''You have helped,'' the girl said, ''and we appreciate it, mister.''

''Well, your father has a funny way of showing his

appreciation.'' Before the girl could reply the sound of approaching riders claimed their attention and they turned to see four riders bearing down on them.

"Know 'em?" Clint asked.

"That's my brother, Cliff, in front," she said, nodding, "with some of our ranch hands. They must be looking for us."

The girl stepped forward to greet her brother, who dismounted swiftly, saying, "What the hell happened, Fran?"

The man appeared to be about twenty-five or -six, five or so years older than his sister.

"We had an accident, Cliff. Pa got pinned under the buckboard and this stranger helped us out."

Cliff examined Clint critically, then grudgingly stepped forward and extended his hand, saying, "We're obliged to you, mister."

"I was just telling your sister that your father has a funny way of showing it."

Cliff gave his sister a puzzled look and she said, "He wanted to check Pa's legs, Cliff."

"You tried to touch my father's legs?" the man asked.

"Only to see if they were damaged."

Cliff looked at his sister and said, "I'll get Pa on one of the horses. Two of the boys will double up, and you ride with me."

He went over to tend to his father, and Clint was still looking to her for some kind of an explanation.

"We really thank you, mister," she said again.

"The name is Clint," he said. "Clint Adams."

"We're grateful for what you did for us, Clint," she told him, "and please don't feel too bad about Pa yelling the way he did. You see, Pa don't like nobody to touch his legs." When Clint still appeared puzzled she said, "He's a cripple, has been for five years now, but he still don't accept it. He just don't like nobody to touch his legs."

"I see," Clint said.

"I'm glad you understand."

Clint watched as Cliff lifted his father easily in his arms and put him astride a horse. The older man's legs did not look quite right; they were stiff, and seemed too thin for a man his size, which at one time must have been considerable.

"Fran," her brother called.

She looked at her brother, then quickly turned back to Clint and said, "Our name's Tyler, mister. We've got the biggest spread in Arizona. If you need anything while you're in these parts, you let us know."

"I only hope the rest of your family feels the same way," he replied.

She was about to answer him, but her brother called out, "Fran, let's get Pa home!" She ran to her brother's horse and he lifted her up behind him.

Clint watched as they rode away, up the rise and beyond, and then gathered up his rope, hung it on his saddle and mounted up. He rode back up to his team and rig and as he climbed aboard and picked up the reins, he realized that the girl had said that her name was Tyler, and the town he was heading for was called Tylerville.

And the Gunsmith was not a firm believer in coincidence.

Chapter Two

Tylerville, Arizona was not a large town, but it was a growing town, and it grew as the Tyler ranch grew. Clint recognized the first fact as he rode in, and came to realize the second fact later.

Badly in need of a drink, he took care of the preliminaries in record time: put Duke and the team up at the livery stable, registered in the hotel, left his gear in his room and sought out the nearest saloon. That the hotel was called the Tyler House, and the saloon was the Tyler Saloon reinforced Clint's opinion about coincidence.

With a cold beer in hand Clint addressed himself to the bartender.

"Met a family called Tyler just outside town," he said to the man. "Any relation to this place?"

"Tyler?" the barkeep said. "Of course. Old man Tyler owns this place."

"And the hotel?"

"Sure," the bartender said. "He practically owns the whole goddamned town."

"I see."

"Who'd you meet up with?" the bartender asked.

"Uh, Fran, I think her name was. Fran Tyler."

"Fran, huh?" the man asked, grinning. "I wouldn't mind meeting up with her, myself."

"And her brother Cliff?"

5

The bartender made a face and said, "Him I can do without."

"You don't like Cliff?"

The man was about to answer, but then his eyes narrowed suspiciously and he backed off.

"I don't like answering questions," he said, instead.

"You could have fooled me," Clint said. He put his empty mug on the bar and asked, "How are you on supplying beer?"

They exchanged glances, and then the bartender took the mug and refilled it. When he brought it back Clint asked him what he thought was an innocent question.

"Who's the sheriff in this town?"

Again the man's eyes narrowed suspiciously. "I said I don't like answering questions. Not about the Tylers. It could be unhealthy."

"I wasn't aware that was a question about the Tylers."

"It is when the sheriff's name is Tyler," the bartender said.

Chapter Three

It was a standing policy of the Gunsmith's to check in with the lawman in every town he entered, just to let them know that he was there. If they recognized his name, they usually appreciated the gesture, and if they didn't, so much the better.

As he entered the sheriff's office there was a man standing at a stove, holding a pot of coffee in his hand, preparing to pour it into a cup he held in his other hand.

"Just in time for coffee," the man said to him.

"Well, that's friendly," Clint said, "and I could use a cup."

The man laughed. "You could use a cup of this for just about anything. Step in and introduce yourself, friend, and I'll find another cup."

"Are you the sheriff?"

"Yep. Sheriff Jack Tyler," the man replied as he searched about for another cup.

He appeared to be in his late thirties; tall and rangy, he gave the impression of being a capable man. A worn Navy Colt rode his right hip.

"Ah, here's another cup," Tyler said. He held it up and examined the inside critically and said, "Uh, I think *I'd* better use this one."

He poured himself a cup, and handed the other to Clint.

"Set yourself down, friend, and introduce yourself," he invited, and sat behind his desk.

Clint sat down in the visitor's chair. "My name is Clint Adams, Sheriff, and all I'm really doing is checking in with you, letting you know that I'm in your town for a short spell."

"Any special reason why I should be inter—Wait a minute," the sheriff said then, as something obviously occurred to him. "I do know that name, don't I?"

"You tell me," Clint said, and tasted the coffee. "God," he said, "You *could* use that for just about anything, couldn't you?"

"Like cleaning a gun," Tyler said. "You're the Gunsmith, ain't you?"

"So I've been told."

"Sure, I've heard of you," Tyler said. "Who hasn't?" Shaking his head he went on, "The Gunsmith, in my town. Well, hell."

Clint took one more sip of the coffee and then put the cup down on the desk.

"That's enough of that," he said, standing up—and mostly he was referring to the coffee. "I just wanted to let you know I was here in Tylerville, Sheriff."

"Well, I sure do appreciate that, Mr. Adams," Tyler said, also standing. "Would you mind telling me how long you intend to stay?"

"Oh, I guess long enough to put a couple of good, hot meals under my belt, and to rest my animals."

"Well, I hope you enjoy our town, then," Sheriff Tyler said.

"Oh, Sheriff, by the way," Clint said, "on my way into town I met a few members of your family."

"Well, there's more than a few," Tyler said. "Which ones did you meet?"

"Your brother, Cliff, your sister, Fran, and your father . . . whose name I never did find out."

"Zack," the lawman said. "Zack Tyler. You just run into them on the road?"

"More or less," Clint said. "I'm sure you'll hear the story from them, so I'll leave it to them to tell it. Thanks for the—uh—coffee. It was an experience."

In fact, it was beginning to look as if Tylerville itself was going to be an experience.

Chapter Four

After his visit to Sheriff Tyler, Clint went looking for one of those hot meals he had mentioned. He found a café on a side street that looked bad enough to be good, and he was right.

After a good, hot lunch he went back to the saloon to cap it off with a cold beer.

"Deputy was looking for you," the bartender said.

"Oh, yeah? For what?"

"Said something about wanting to try out your gun."

"What?"

"That's what he said."

Just what he needed, an overeager deputy out to make a name for himself. "What else did he say?"

"That's all," the bartender said, looking nervous. "That's all I was supposed to tell you."

"What do you mean all you were supposed to tell me?" Clint asked. "Who put you up to it?"

"The deputy."

"What's this deputy's name?"

"Joe."

"Joe what?"

"Bags," a voice said from behind him, before the bartender could answer. Clint recognized the voice, and suddenly his memory went flying back some years. . . .

• • •

It had been right after the business in Mexico, when Clint had finally put his old memories of Jenny Sand to rest.* He had met Joe Bags, a young would-be gunman who was awed by the Gunsmith legend and reputation, and was hoping to ride with Clint, thereby making a name for himself.

Later, in a saloon in Texas, Clint told Bags his travel plans.

"I'll ride along," Bags had said.

"No, I don't think so, Bags," Clint had said.

"Why not?"

"You make me nervous. I'm not going to be anybody's reputation-maker. Come morning I'll go my way and you go yours."

He had put down his drink and said, "I can't do that, Clint. Oh, you're right. I did latch onto you because I figured that was the surest way to a reputation, but you were a big disappointment to me. After spending so much time with you I don't think you're all that good. You think too much before drawing your gun, and don't think I believed all that stuff about not playing with your gun," he had told the Gunsmith. "You wouldn't shoot targets with me because you were afraid I'd show you up."

"If that's what you want to believe, kid, go ahead," Clint had told him.

"Don't hand me that shit," Bags had snapped, standing up and knocking his chair over. "I'm saying you're yella!"

Clint had been afraid of that, ever since meeting the young Joe Bags. Realizing that he wasn't going to ride Clint Adams to a rep, Bags figured that the only other way to get what he wanted was to outdraw the Gunsmith.

"Don't do this, Bags," Clint had told him. "It's not worth it."

"Outside, Adams, Mr. Gunsmith Clint Adams," Bags

*The Gunsmith #3: The Woman Hunt.

had said loudly, making damn sure that everyone in the room knew who Clint was. "I'll be waiting for you outside."

Bags had stormed out of the saloon.

What neither man had noticed were the three men seated at a corner table taking the conversation in with great interest, especially when they heard who Clint was.

"This is our chance to make a name for ourselves, boys," one man said. "All we got to do is kill the Gunsmith."

"You make it sound damn easy," one of the other men said.

"It is," the first man replied. "Let's go outside fast, before the Gunsmith does. We'll be waiting for him along with that other fella. Between the four of us, we ought to be able to gun 'im, and then all we got to do is kill the other fella."

The speaker rose and the other two men followed him outside in a big hurry.

Clint may not have noticed the three men while he was talking to Joe Bags, but he noticed them leaving the saloon in a hurry, and didn't like it one bit.

When Joe Bags saw the three coming out of the saloon, he didn't much like it, either.

"You fellas figure on being an audience?" he asked as they approached him.

"Audience hell, friend. We figure if you got a beef with the Gunsmith, you could use all the help you kin get," the spokesman for the three men said.

"That's where you're wrong, friend," Bags said. "I don't need any help at all."

"Well, we figure on dealing ourselves into this hand, anyway," the man said.

Bags saw Clint come out of the saloon and realized what was happening.

"Joe," Clint called out, "you got some friends on your side, now?"

"They're no friends of mine, Clint," Bags replied. "They're just looking to make a name for themselves."

"Like you are?"

"Like I was," Bags said. "I'm calling it off, Clint. In fact, I'm walking over to your side of the street."

"Hey, what the hell—" one of the other men said.

"Joe, why don't you just step out of the street," Clint called out. He saw an opportunity to give Joe Bags something else that he'd been wanting, a chance to see the Gunsmith in action—if he failed to back the three men down, that is.

Bags stared at Clint for a moment to see if he was serious and then, realizing that he was, walked off the street and up onto the boardwalk.

The three men were lined up with the spokesman standing in the middle, and the other two were looking to him for guidance now.

"We can still take him," the man told them. "We're all pretty good with our guns."

As if he had been able to read their lips, Clint Adams called out, "Now you boys might all be pretty good with your guns, but you've got to know that one of you is going to die." He paused for effect and then asked, "Which one of you will it be?"

Slowly, one by one, they walked off the street, with their spokesman being the last to leave. As if achieving some small accomplishment, he fixed the Gunsmith with a malevolent glare as he followed his partners off the street. All three men mounted up and rode out of town.

Joe Bags had come up behind Clint as the Gunsmith watched the three men ride out.

"I still haven't gotten a chance to really see you in action," he said, "and you know something? I'm damn glad I didn't."

"Turn around, Clint," Bags said.

Clint turned, wondering if three years or so had mel-

lowed Joe Bags, or did the younger man regret his decision not to try the Gunsmith when he had the chance?

When he saw the grin on Bags's face, he knew that all
of those thoughts were gone for good, and he was glad.

Chapter Five

Bags had filled out some; his face and upper torso were heavier looking than Clint remembered.

"Hello, Clint," he said. Shrugging his shoulders he looked past the Gunsmith at the bartender, then back at Clint and said, "I couldn't resist a little joke."

"Sure," Clint said. "Same old Bags, huh?"

"Not really," Bags said, seriously. "There are some definite differences. Buy you a drink?"

"Well," Clint said, "now there's a difference, right there!"

Bags asked the bartender for two beers, and then he and Clint walked to a back table from which they could see the entire room.

"That's something new," Clint said, indicating the badge on Bags's chest.

"I've been wearing it about four months, now," Bags said, "but I intend to trade it in pretty soon."

"For what?"

"For one that says 'sheriff' without the 'deputy,' " Bags said. "Election's coming up pretty soon."

"Sheriff's name is Tyler, isn't it?" Clint asked.

"That's right."

"And you're going to run against him, in Tylerville?"

Clint asked. "Have you thought this all the way through, Joe?"

"I have, yes," Bags said. "But to tell you the truth, I didn't really decide until earlier today, when I saw you ride into town on that big black of yours."

"How does that affect your decision?"

"It gives me the one thing I didn't have before," Bags said.

"What's that?"

"Somebody to watch my back."

Clint lifted his mug and drank some of the beer, thinking over what Bags had just said.

"I know that running against Tyler is not going to make me a popular man," Bags said, "especially with the other Tylers, but I think I have a real chance, Clint. I think a lot of the people in this town are tired of being under the thumb of old Zack Tyler and his sons."

"Sheriff Tyler strikes me as being a pretty decent fella," Clint said. "He presents a good image anyway."

"Oh, he's got the looks and the charm, all right, and he'll get a lot of votes for that, but as for being sheriff, he only does as much as his old man will let him. If I win, I'll be my own man, Clint."

"And you think that's what this town needs?" Clint asked.

"Definitely," Bags said. "But like I said, I need someone to watch my back while I'm campaigning." Bags held up his hand quickly and said, "Don't decide right now, Clint. Think it over. Stay around until tomorrow and give me your answer then."

"Well, I had intended to rest up over night," Clint said, "maybe find a poker game."

"That'll be no problem," Bags said. "Just stay around here and a game will find you."

"All right, Joe," Clint said. "I'll think it over."

"I can't offer you any money, Clint—"

Now it was Clint's turn to hold up his hand. "What I'm thinking over is whether or not I want to do you a favor," he said. "I never had any thought of money."

"I appreciate that."

"Tell me what happened after we split up in Texas," Clint said, and they spent the next hour or so catching up.

"You've given up the idea of making a rep as a gunman?" Clint asked.

"Oh, yeah, but even that was just recent," Bags said.

"What changed your mind?"

"Bill Hickok," Bags said, and Clint's stomach jumped, as it always did when someone mentioned his dead friend. "Him getting shot in the back like that," Bags went on. "If he hadn't been Wild Bill Hickok, that wouldn't have happened."

"Probably not," Clint agreed, soberly.

"That made me give up the idea of making a name for myself with a gun," Bags said, "so I decided to try and do it with a badge."

So, Clint thought, *the desire for a rep hasn't changed, just the method by which it would be achieved.*

"Making a name with a badge can be just as dangerous as making one with a gun, Joe," Clint said. Having done both, the Gunsmith was speaking from personal experience.

"Can't just go through life being a nobody, Clint," Bags said, "It just ain't in me."

Clint examined his young friend, then decided not to try and argue him out of it. The law wasn't a bad profession to pursue, and it was better than being a gunman, killing just to make a name for yourself.

They had one more drink together and then the deputy went off to perform his rounds. As Joe predicted, a poker game came along and found Clint, and he stopped drinking and played some aggressive poker with some overmatched townspeople.

"I think that will about do it for tonight, gentlemen," he finally decided, late that night.

"You've got a lot of my money there, son," a white-haired man said, frowning.

Clint looked up at the bartender, who appeared to be closing up and said, "Tomorrow's another day, friend. Bartender looks like he's getting ready to shut down."

"That never stopped us," the man said, looking at the other men at the table. The man looked back at Clint and said, "I've got a big back room behind my shop, with a large round table."

Clint realized that he was being invited to play in a little different kind of game than he'd just played—or maybe *invited* was too nice a word for it.

"I don't think so, friend," he said. "I just rode into town today, and the miles are starting to gang up on me."

The man fixed him with a cold stare and asked, "Are you saying you don't want to give us a chance to get our money back?"

Clint returned the man's stare with one of his own, a few degrees colder. "Not tonight, my friend. Another time."

"Look, mister—"

"Don't push it," Clint said, cutting him off. He addressed the other players and said, "If any of you gentlemen are here tomorrow night, I'd be happy to sit down with you again."

The three other men exchanged glances, and then one of them said, "That suits us, mister."

"Fine."

"I'll be here tomorrow, too," the white-haired man said. Clint studied him a little closer now, and saw that the white hair was not an indication of age, but perhaps of a hard life. Still, a hard life was no excuse for bad manners, or poor losing.

"I won't play with you again, friend," Clint said, "and I wouldn't advise that you try and press the matter." Clint turned away from the man and said to the others, ''Good night.''

In leaving, Clint kept a wary eye on the man until he was out the door, and kept his eyes and ears open on the way to the hotel.

There weren't too many things worse—or more dangerous—than a bad loser.

Chapter Six

When Clint came down for breakfast the next morning, Joe Bags was waiting in the lobby for him.

"Morning," Clint said.

"Good morning," Bags replied. "I thought it might be a good idea for us to have breakfast together."

"You did, huh?" Clint asked. He headed for the hotel dining room with Bags close on his heels.

"I thought it might be a good idea," Bags repeated.

"You sure you're not just in a hurry to find out my answer?" Clint asked.

"Answer to what?" Bags asked, contriving to look innocent.

"Bags," Clint said, turning to face the deputy, "don't ever do that."

"Do what?"

"Plaster innocence all over your face that way," Clint answered. "It just isn't a good fit, and it looks so out of place."

Bags frowned at Clint, and the Gunsmith said, "Now that's better," and continued on to the dining room.

"Clint, come on, now," Bags said, hurrying after him. "I admit it, I'm anxious to hear your answer."

"Have I ever refused to do a favor for a friend?" Clint asked over his shoulder.

"Well, I ain't seen you for some years," Bags said,

"and I didn't know you before then, so why don't you tell me the answer to that one?"

"The answer is no," Clint said.

He sat down at an empty table from which he could see the entire room, and Bags sat across from him.

"No you ain't never refused to do a favor for a friend, or no you won't help me?"

"No to the first part, and yes to the second."

Bags frowned, thought it over and once he had it sorted out, smiled.

"I appreciate this, Clint."

"Don't mention it," Clint said. "Let's eat breakfast."

When they had finished breakfast and were chasing it down with a pot of coffee Clint said, "I played some poker last night with some men whose names I didn't get, and one of them was a pretty sore loser."

"Big fella, too young for the white hair he's carrying around? Mean face?"

"That's him."

"He's not only a sore loser, Clint, he's a bad one," Bags said. "He's in jail every Saturday night for breaking somebody's jaw—and sometimes it's a fella he's beat at poker!"

"What's his name and claim to fame?" Clint asked. "He said something about a store with a back room."

"He owns the general store and sometimes runs a poker game in the back room."

"He tried to rope me into a game last night, when the saloon was closing up."

"And you told him no?"

"I told him no last night, and I told him I wouldn't ever play him again."

"That must have gotten him sore," Bags said. "He's no gunman, Clint, but I'd watch out for him just the same. He's mean, and he'll look for a way to get back at you."

"Let him look," Clint said. "What else has he got besides a bad streak and a hardware store?"

Bags's eyes lit up and he said, "He's got a blond wife that turns heads every time she walks down the street."

"Is that so?" Clint asked, with interest. Rubbing his jaw he said, "Maybe I turned down his poker game too soon."

"Don't go messing with his wife, Clint," Bags said. "You'll only get him madder at you."

"I guess you notice how concerned I am about that," Clint said. "You haven't told me this fella's name yet. It isn't a name I'd recognize, is it?"

"Hell, no," Bags said. "I don't think he's ever been out of Tylerville. He's just sort of a town tough. Name's Frank Bell and his wife's name is Edie."

"Edie Bell?"

"That's her."

"I've never heard of her, either," Clint said.

"Take my advice," Joe Bags said as his friend stood up, "keep it that way."

"In case you haven't noticed," Clint said, "I'm older than you, so I'm the one who should be handing out the advice."

"Well," Bags said, also standing, "I don't remember you being the type to go out of your way to get people mad at you."

"I'm not," Clint said, "but somehow when you win at poker, you always manage to get somebody mad, and you can't be worrying about it."

"That your advice?"

"That's it for today," Clint said. "See me tomorrow for more words of wisdom. Don't you have rounds to do, or something?"

"I thought maybe we'd talk some about my campaign."

"I thought you wanted me to cover your back," Clint said, "not plan your campaign."

"Well, I figure since you been through it before . . ."

Clint stared at his friend, then said, "All right, come

on. I'll walk your rounds with you, and we can discuss it.''

During rounds Clint asked, "Who have you spoken to regarding your, uh, campaign?"

"Just you," Bags said. "It's been in the back of my mind for a long time, though. Seeing you ride into town just sort of pushed it to the front."

"What's led you to believe that you have a chance against Tyler?"

Bags shrugged and said, "just keeping my ears open and listening to what people have to say when they think no one is listening."

"A man can get into a lot of trouble that way," Clint said.

"What way?"

"Listening to what people don't want him to hear."

Chapter Seven

While Clint Adams was making rounds with Deputy Joe Bags, Sheriff Jack Tyler was riding through the front gates of the Big T Ranch, owned and built by his father, Zack Tyler. Someday—Zack was fond of saying—it would all be Jack's, but right now the thirty-year-old, eldest Tyler son had to be content with being Sheriff and running the town. That was the way the old man put it, but the truth was the old man ran everything within a hundred mile radius.

Jack reined his horse in at the house and gave him over to one of the hands.

"Keep him ready, Leo," he said. "I may be leaving at any moment."

Leo knew what that meant. If the old man started in on Jack again, that would be notice enough for the sheriff to head back to town.

As Jack Tyler entered the house the first person he saw was his sister, Fran.

"Where's Cliff?" he asked, as if she were a servant in the house instead of one of the residents. In fact, she was carrying a tray of food which was obviously meant for the old man.

"He went out early, Jack. I don't know where. You'll have to ask one of the hands."

"Is that for the old man?"

"Yes."

"Give it to him and then come back down. I want to talk to you about what happened yesterday."

"On the road?"

"Go up and give him the tray," Jack said. "I assume he still has use of the arms and can feed himself?"

"Jack—"

"Go on, Fran. I'll wait for you in the living room."

He went into the largest room in the house and poured himself a drink while he waited for his sister. Cliff was probably out playing foreman, a job that had been Jack's until he had been elected—with the help of old Zack— sheriff of Tylerville.

"Isn't it a little early for that?" Fran asked as she entered the room.

"You tell that to the old man?"

"Ha," she said, "you know nobody tells Pa anything."

"Yeah," he said, pouring himself a second drink. "Tell me what happened on the road yesterday."

"We overturned," she said, and continued on until she'd explained the entire incident. "Where did you hear about it?"

"In town," he said.

"From who?"

"Clint Adams."

"Oh, really?" she asked, looking interested. "Didn't he tell you the whole story?"

"He told me that he'd met you on the road," Jack said. "I came out here to find out all the details." He put down his empty glass and turned away from the bar to face his sister.

"Do you know who that man was?"

"Clint Adams, isn't it?"

"Clint Adams, yeah," Jack said, "but they call him the Gunsmith!"

"The lawman?"

"The gunfighter," Jack said. "I want to know what he's doing in my town, Fran."

"Your town?" she asked, but he ignored the remark.

"I want to know, Fran."

"So, why tell me?"

"I want you to go to town and thank Mr. Adams for helping you and Pa," he said.

"Since when do you care about Pa?" she asked. "Or me?"

He walked over to her and laid his palm against her cheek very softly.

"You know, Fran, Pa can't last forever," he said quietly, "and when he dies, this place will be mine."

"Yours," she said, "and Cliff's, and Ben's."

At twenty-five Ben was the youngest of the three Tyler boys and two years older than Fran.

"Where is my little brother, by the way?" he asked.

"He went out with Cliff."

"Those two have gotten pretty tight lately, haven't they?" he asked.

"Why not?" she asked. "You never made any effort."

"I don't need anybody, Fran," Jack said.

"I know," she said.

She did, though, and nobody ever seemed to think of that. Jack was out for himself, Cliff and Ben were joining forces to get what they wanted, and the old man was as tightfisted as ever, hanging onto what he had, to what he'd built, keeping his sons on a string by giving them each a little something to keep them busy.

What did she have?

"Come into town as soon as possible, Fran," Jack said, "and thank the man. I'll be watching for you."

"Sure, Jack," she said.

Her oldest brother nodded, then turned and left her there without saying good-bye. She followed him out and caught him before he went out the front door.

"Don't you want to go upstairs and see how Pa is?"

"Why?" he asked. "I already know how he is. Mean and ornery, like always."

"His legs—" she started to say.

"He was mean before his legs ever got hurt, Fran," he reminded her. "I don't know why you keep making excuses for him. He don't treat you any better than he treats us."

"Neither do you," she said, turning away and walking to the kitchen.

Jack Tyler stood there for a few seconds, staring at the door his sister had gone through, then shrugged and walked out. What did she expect? he thought. If he didn't think about himself, who the hell would?

Cliff and Ben Tyler came riding up on the house from behind just as their older brother was leaving.

"I wonder what the *sheriff* wanted?" Cliff said sarcastically.

"Who knows?" Ben asked. "He doesn't usually come around unless the old man sends for him."

"Think he did?"

"What for? He and the old man have very little to say to each other."

"The old man don't talk to none of us much anymore," Cliff said.

"'Cept Fran," Ben observed.

"Yeah, but that's only to tell her what he wants to eat," Cliff said. "Pretty soon, though, the old man won't be telling any of us anything anymore."

When Sheriff Jack Tyler rode back into town he spotted Joe Bags doing his rounds, and saw that Clint Adams was walking with the deputy. The two men were deep in conversation, and Tyler had a feeling that they hadn't just met recently.

He left his horse at the livery stable and went back to his

office, where he pulled a bottle of whiskey out of the bottom drawer of his desk.

Maybe, he thought, he wouldn't have to wait for Fran to find out what the Gunsmith was doing in his town.

Chapter Eight

"What's up, Sheriff?" Bags asked Tyler. "I heard you wanted to see me."

"Sit down, Joe," Tyler said. "Drink?"

"No, thanks." Bags took a seat.

He watched as Tyler took a deep swallow from the whiskey bottle, and then capped it.

"I want to talk to you about a man who came into town yesterday. Clint Adams."

"What about him?"

"Do you know him?"

"Sure, I know him."

"No, I mean before he came to town, did you know him?"

"We've met before," Bags said. "It was a few years back."

"Are you friends?"

"I don't know if we're friends, exactly," Joe Bags said. He thought back and remembered having said and done some pretty stupid things. He wouldn't go around claiming that Clint Adams was his friend until Clint told him it was so.

"But you know each other?"

"Sure, I said so, didn't I?"

"Yeah, you did," Tyler said.

Bags waited a few beats, and then asked, "So what about him?"

"Oh, I was just wondering what he was doing in my—in town," Tyler said. "You wouldn't know, would you?"

"All I know is what he told me," Bags said. "He's passing through."

"That's all?"

"That's it," Bags said.

Bags didn't like Tyler much. On the outside, Tyler appeared to be mild mannered and friendly, but Bags knew that down deep the man was mean—the way Bags had heard his old man was mean.

"People like the Gunsmith don't just pass through a town," Tyler said. "He's got something on his mind."

He didn't when he got here, Bags thought, but he said, "Nothing that I know of."

"Well, maybe he'll say something," Tyler said. "If he does, you can let me know, can't you?"

"I could," Bags said.

The tone of Bags's voice went right over Tyler's head, and he said, "Good. Now that that's settled, you can go to work. Keep an eye on Adams, Joe. That's part of your job, too—if you want to keep it, that is."

"Oh, I want to keep it," Bags said, as he started for the door.

"Good," Tyler said. "Just keep doing like you're told, and you'll get to keep it."

Sure, Bags thought, *I want the job—just long enough to stick around and get yours.*

Chapter Nine

Bags found Clint in the saloon, having a midday beer. He got one for himself, and then joined the Gunsmith at his table.

"Back already?"

They had still been walking Bags's rounds together when a kid came running up and told the deputy that the sheriff wanted to see him.

"He wanted to ask me about you," Bags said. "If I knew you, if I knew what you were doing in town."

"What'd you tell him?"

"Well, I didn't tell him anything about my wanting to run for sheriff," Bags said. "I told him you were just passing through."

"He bought that?"

"Well, except for my asking you to do me a favor, it's true," Bags pointed out.

"Tell me about Tyler," Clint said. "From what I saw, he's too good to be true. He's handsome, charming, friendly—"

"He's mean," Bags said. "The rest is just an act."

"I thought as much."

"You know something?" Bags said. "Tyler talked to me once about becoming sheriff. He said that the old man could have 'appointed' him sheriff, he's got that much power, but he also said that he rejected that. He ran for office and won on his own.''

''He really believes that?'' Clint asked.

''Yeah, he really does. I don't know whether it's true or not, but I'll tell you one thing. It could be. I think Tyler could have run on his own and won, but I'm gonna beat him, Clint.''

''What if his old man appoints him this time?''

''I've thought about that,'' Bags admitted. ''If Jack Tyler was telling the truth, if he really rejected his father's help the first time, he'll do it again—and that's how I'll beat him.''

''From what I've heard about Zack Tyler while I've been in town,'' Clint said, ''I don't think he'd sit still while his son lost the election for sheriff. He wants a Tyler to be wearing the badge.''

''You been listening to people talk?'' Bags asked him. ''I thought you told me that was dangerous.''

''It's also very informative. When do you intend to announce your candidacy?'' Clint asked.

''There's a meeting of the city council tomorrow, as a matter of fact,'' Bags said. ''I'll make the announcement there.''

''Will Tyler be there?''

''I'm sure he will,'' Bags said. ''Do you think they'll let him fire me when he finds out—''

''I don't think he would,'' Clint broke in. ''It wouldn't do him any good at the polls, when the time comes.''

''I suppose not.''

''You better be ready for what happens after you make the announcement, Bags,'' Clint said. ''Zack Tyler won't take it too kindly.''

''Oh, I know that.''

''You picked a hell of a place to start your career as a lawman,'' Clint said.

''Well, if it came easy, it wouldn't be worth anything, would it?'' Bags asked.

''No, it wouldn't,'' Clint replied, thinking that Joe Bags had changed quite a bit since they had last seen each other. Quite a bit, indeed.

Chapter Ten

The next day, Clint found some work to keep him busy while waiting for Bags to come out of the council meeting. He was in his wagon, working on a .45 that needed a new firing pin when Bags knocked on the outside.

"Come on in," Clint called out, knowing who it was.

Bags climbed in the back and sat down on a stool.

"So?" Clint asked, putting the gun down.

"I made the announcement," Bags said.

"And?"

"Well, the council accepted the announcement pretty well," Bags said.

"And Tyler?"

Bags hesitated a moment, and Clint saw the color mounting in the man's face.

"He thought it was funny," Bags finally said. "He laughed, and said he thought it was funny."

"Let him laugh," Clint said.

"God, I wanted to smash his face in," Bags said tightly. "I wanted to wipe that smug look—"

"Was he charming about it?"

"Was he?" Bags said. "He made a couple of jokes and even had a few members of the council laughing along with him."

"Well, they won't be laughing when you beat him," Clint said.

"I hope not," Bags said.

"You're not having second thoughts, are you?"

Bags hesitated, then said, "Maybe."

"Well, it's too late to back out now," Clint said. "You're in it."

"I know it, but Tyler is so confident. He stopped me outside and said that after he won he'd still keep me on as his deputy."

"That's generous of him."

"That's his meanness coming through, like I told you," Bags said.

"I've got some advice for you, my friend," Clint said, "now that your intentions are out in the open. Find out who your friends are. Find out if you have any in this town. Walk around today and talk to people, find out who's behind you and who you can count on."

"To cover me?" Bags said. "You're the only one—"

"Not to cover you, Bags," Clint said. "For something even more important than that. Find out who you can count on for votes."

"Oh."

"Because if you find out that you're wrong, and that you can't count on anyone, there's no shame in pulling out."

"If I did that I'd have to pull out of this town," Bags said.

"Well, that might not be such a bad idea," Clint said, "but you can cross that bridge when you come to it. Right now just go out there and find out where you stand."

"Right," Bags said, and he got up so fast that he banged his head on the shelf he'd been sitting under.

"And don't always count on me to watch your back," Clint said, "or your head. Right?"

Grinning sheepishly, Bags said, "Right."

It wasn't really time yet to start worrying about the deputy's back. Old Zack Tyler didn't know yet that Bags was planning on running against his son in the election.

Someone on the council would make sure that the old man found out, but that would take a while.

It would probably be a matter of hours, and maybe a day, before Zack would react to the news that someone was going to run against his son. It would be interesting to see what the old man's first move would be. Would he try to buy Bags off, or simply try to run him out of town?

Being a wealthy man, his first thought might be to offer Bags money, and Clint wasn't so sure that, if he were Bags's age and in Bags's position—depending on the amount of money involved—he himself wouldn't just take the money and forget about being a lawman.

Chapter Eleven

Cyrus Tidyman was mayor of Tylerville, but he was also Zack Tyler's representative on the Tylerville City Council. He kept Tyler informed of all the business the council discussed, and when he learned of the deputy's intention of running against Jack Tyler for sheriff in the next election, he immediately had his buggy hitched and rode out to the Big T.

He was too afraid of old Zack not to.

Tidyman stopped his buggy right in front of the house, mounted the porch and knocked.

"I'd like to talk to your father, Miss Fran," he said when Fran Tyler answered the door.

"Come in, Mr. Mayor," she said. "I'll go up and tell Pa you're here."

Fran left Mayor Tidyman standing in the hall because she didn't like him, rather than offer him a chair somewhere, and went up to announce him.

She knocked on her father's bedroom door and when he called out she entered.

"What is it?" he asked, irritably.

"The mayor is here to see you, Pa."

"Send him up then, girl."

"Yes, Pa."

When the mayor entered old Zack's room the old man was sitting up in bed with two pillows behind him. Every time Tidyman saw Zack Tyler he marveled at how much older the man looked than the last time he'd seen him, even if it had only been one day. In this case, it had been almost a week and Zack looked as if he'd aged ten years.

"I heard about your accident, Zack," Tidyman said. "I'm glad you weren't hurt bad."

"You're a liar, Cyrus," Zack Tyler said. "You wish I'd been killed, just like the rest of the people around me do, but I'm too damned ornery to die, and you all know it."

"Zack—"

"Shut up and tell me why you're here," Zack said.

Even laid up in bed like that, with legs that would never allow him to stand again, Zack Tyler still intimidated Cyrus Tidyman, and Tidyman hated him—and himself—for that.

"I thought you'd want to know that we discussed the upcoming elections for sheriff."

"And?" Zack asked. "Was anybody foolish enough to announce that they would oppose my boy for the job?"

"Well, yes, someone was—"

"Who?" Zack boomed. He had not expected such an answer to his question. In fact, his question had not even been serious.

"His deputy."

"His deputy?" Zack repeated. "What the hell is his name?"

"Bags, Joe Bags."

"Bags? What the hell kind of name is that?" the old man demanded.

"Well, I don't rightly—"

"How long has this Bags been Jack's deputy?"

"A few months."

"Does he have any background in the law?

"Not that I know of."

"Does he have a chance to beat Jack fair and square?"

"Jack doesn't think so," Tidyman said. "He laughed when the man announced his candidacy."

"He didn't accept my help last time," Zack said, his tone clearly indicating that he thought Jack Tyler a fool for that, "and he might not this time. I want to know if this man has a chance to beat my son in the election."

"I don't know—"

"Well then, find out, damn it!" Zack said.

"All right."

"If he does, tell Jack to fire him."

"Jack doesn't listen to me, Zack," Tidyman said, "You know that."

"Of course he doesn't," Zack Tyler told the little man. "He doesn't respect you any more than I do."

"Zack—"

"Go on, get out of here, Cyrus," Zack said. "Find out how much of a chance this Joe Bags has of winning the election, and then come back."

"All right, Zack," Tidyman said. He fiddled with his hat for a few moments, then abruptly pressed it down on his head and backed out of the room.

"Fran!" Zack Tyler shouted at the top of his lungs. "Damn it, Fran!"

"I'm coming, Pa!" he heard his daughter call from the hallway. She came into the room breathlessly and said, "I was showing the mayor out."

"I know the man's a goddamned incompetent," Zack said, "but I'm sure he could have found the door all by himself."

"Yes, Pa."

"I want you to get me Jack," Zack instructed her.

"He was here yesterday—"

"Why didn't he come up and see me?"

"I don't know, Pa—"

"Well send somebody to town—no, go to town yourself and tell him I want to see him, and do it now."

"What about your lunch?"

"Lunch be damned!" the old man shouted. "Do what I tell you, girl, and do it now!"

"Yes, Pa."

"Go on!"

She backed out of the room, closing the door behind her. Most of the people who ever entered that room backed out, as if they suspected that the old man was faking his inability to use his legs and would spring at them the moment their back was turned.

It was testimony to the amount of fear old Zack still generated, even as an invalid.

Chapter Twelve

Clint Adams was standing on the boardwalk in front of the hotel when Fran Tyler rode into town on a big dapple gray. He admired the way she sat the horse, with her back straight and her chest thrust out. He watched as she directed her horse over to the sheriff's office, then climbed down, secured the animal, and went in.

Knowing that she wouldn't find her brother there, because he had seen Jack Tyler leave his office only moments before, Clint left the boardwalk and crossed the street to the jail.

He walked in without knocking, saying, "Deputy—" and stopping short, as if surprised not to find the deputy there.

Fran Tyler's face also reflected surprise, although hers was genuine, as she turned quickly and saw Clint standing there. Her very dark hair was tied behind her with a bow and he took the opportunity to examine her face more closely than he had the last time they met.

She had wide brown eyes, high, prominent cheekbones that hinted at the possibility of some Indian blood in her. Dark skin also added to that possibility. Her mouth was wide and full, and opened now in surprise. Her teeth were even and very white, and she ran her tongue over the bottom ones.

"You startled me," she said.

47

"I'm sorry."

She was wearing riding clothes, which included a buck-skin skirt and high boots, so that there was only a very thin strip of brown flesh showing between the two.

"I came to see my brother," she said.

"The sheriff," he replied. "I saw him leave the office just a little while ago. I was looking for the deputy, myself."

"I see."

"Maybe we should wait together," Clint suggested.

"No," Fran said quickly.

"Well, then, maybe you should allow me to buy you some coffee, and then we can check back later."

Fran hesitated, then said, "All right."

She didn't want Clint Adams there when her brother Jack came back, because she didn't want Jack to think that she was going to do what he had told her to do the day before. She had decided that if the sheriff wanted to know what the Gunsmith was doing in town, he should ask him himself. That was his job, and she'd be damned if she was going to do it for him.

"The hotel dining room okay?" he asked as they left the office.

"It's fine."

When they were seated at a table he asked, "Would you like something to eat? Some lunch?"

"Just coffee," she said.

Clint told the waitress to bring a pot of coffee and two cups.

"How's your father?" Clint asked.

"He's fine, thank you," she said. "I, uh, should thank you again for what you did—"

"That's not necessary," he assured her.

"Well," she said, "thanks, anyway."

"I've been hearing a lot about your ranch and your father since I've been in town," he told her.

"You can probably believe most of it," she said.

"Then I'm impressed."

"Don't be," she said, but she didn't elaborate.

The coffee came at that point and he remained quiet while the waitress put down the pot and the two cups, and then poured.

When she left Clint reached out and touched the back of Fran's hand with his forefinger.

"You're much darker than your father and your brothers," he said.

She looked down and rubbed her hand where he had touched it. "My mother was Navaho," she said. "My three brothers are actually only half brothers."

"Interesting," he said.

"Actually, Jack and the others, Cliff and Ben, are also half brothers. Jack's mother died in childbirth, and then Pa married again and had Cliff and Ben. When their mother died he married my mother, and they had me."

"Are you all . . . close?"

The look on her face answered the question before she even had a chance to speak.

"Not likely," she said. "Cliff and Ben are the only ones who are close, maybe because they're full brothers."

"Doesn't exactly sound like the perfect family situation," Clint said, adding, "if you don't mind my saying so."

"Hell, no, I don't mind," she said. She picked up her cup and sipped the coffee, and Clint did the same. Fran wrinkled her nose, but the coffee was the way Clint liked it, strong.

"Would you like something else?" he asked her.

"No, not really," she said. "I just have to talk to Jack for Pa, is all, and I'd like to get it over with." She started to get up, saying, "Maybe I'll just go over there and wait for him."

"Maybe you should," Clint said, "because you don't seem to be all that comfortable here."

She stopped short and said, "What does that mean?"

"Just that you seem to be uncomfortable—or nervous—here with me," he explained.

"You don't make me nervous, Mr. Adams," she said, going on the defensive. "I just have some other things on my mind."

"Well, then, what do you say we get together sometime when you don't have other things on your mind."

"Like when?"

"I don't know. How about tomorrow afternoon?"

"Where?" she asked, frowning.

"Someplace neutral," he said. "We'll get a basket of food from the hotel and go on a picnic somewhere."

"A picnic?"

"Sure. What's the matter, you don't like picnics?"

"Of course I like picnics."

"You just don't want to go on one with me, is that it?"

"That's not it at all—"

"Fine then. I'll get the basket together and come out to the ranch tomorrow afternoon and pick you up."

"Uh, I don't think—"

"It's settled," Clint said. "You better go and talk to your brother, before he gets too hard to find."

"Yeah, maybe I better," she said.

"I'll see you tomorrow, Fran," he said. "I can call you Fran, can't I?"

"Sure."

"And you can call me Clint."

"Fine . . . Clint. I'll see you tomorrow."

He watched her leave, then poured himself a second cup of coffee, feeling very satisfied with himself.

Chapter Thirteen

Fran Tyler was feeling rather confused as she walked back across the street to the sheriff's office. She had the feeling she had been manipulated into something. She also had the feeling she should be angry about it . . . but she wasn't.

As she entered the office Jack Tyler was pouring himself a cup of coffee.

"Ah," he said when he saw her, "the little squaw."

When they were younger—when she was a very little girl, as a matter of fact—Jack would call her that, but it was almost with affection, then. Now, and for the past ten years or so, it always sounded like an insult.

"Hello, Jack."

"You didn't come to town yesterday like I told you," he said.

"Asked," she said. "You asked me to come to town."

He laughed and said, "I never asked a woman to do anything in my life."

"That's probably why you're not married," she said.

"I'm not married because I don't want to be," he said. "Why'd you come to town today, little sister? To do what I *told* you?"

"No," she said. "Pa wants to see you."

"Ha!" he said, sitting down with his coffee cup in hand. "He sent you to fetch me?"

"He sent me to tell you that he'd like to see you."

"Bullspit! He's *telling* me to go and see him."

"Is that like you telling me—"

"No, there's a difference," he said. "Women are born to be told what to do by a man. I'm the sheriff of this town. Zack Tyler and nobody else tells me what to do."

"No," she said, "I'll bet."

He gave her a sharp look and she backed off a couple of steps. She had felt the sting of the hands of the Tyler men on enough occasions in the past. Her face still stung when she thought about the last time Jack had slapped her.

"Is that all?" Jack asked.

"Yes, that's it."

"Are you gonna go over and talk to Clint Adams now?"

"No," she said, taking another backward step. "I'm not."

He stared at her for a few moments, and then he said, "To hell with you, then. I don't need you. Get out, Fran."

"With pleasure," she said. She started for the door, but he called out again before she reached it.

"Fran!"

"What?"

"Tell the old man I'll be out to see him later on."

"Sure," she said, knowingly.

"Official business," Jack added.

"Of course," Fran said. "What other reason could there possibly be?"

Chapter Fourteen

Whatever the reason was, two hours later Sheriff Jack Tyler rode up to the main house of the Big T and dismounted.

"Keep him available," Jack Tyler told Leo.

The sheriff walked into the house and went right up the steps to the old man's room. He didn't even see Fran come out of the kitchen and watch him go up.

When Jack Tyler stalked into the room, Zack looked up and said, "What kept you?"

"I'm a busy man, Pa," the sheriff said.

"Bullspit! Next time I call, you come running a lot faster than you just did, boy. You hear?"

"You want something from me, old man, or do you just want to fight?"

"Fight," the old man said. "When was the last time you ever gave me a real fight, boy?"

"I knew it," Jack said, and started to leave.

"Wait a minute!" Zack shouted.

"If you've got something to say, then say it, old man."

"All right, boy," he said, "we won't fight—this time. I hear that you're going to have some competition in the next election."

Jack Tyler laughed and said, "Then you hear wrong."

"Your deputy—what's his name? Bags?—isn't planning on running against you?"

"Oh, he's planning on it, all right," the sheriff said, "but he hasn't got a chance to beat me."

"You don't think so, eh?"

"No, I don't. Why, do you?"

"There's always a chance."

"Not this time."

"You don't need my help, then?"

Sheriff Tyler narrowed his eyes and said, "I didn't need it last time and I don't need it this time."

"Have it your way then, boy," Zack said, "but take my advice. Fire this fella now."

"Your brain is starting to go, old man," Jack said. "That wouldn't look good at all. No, not only don't I plan to fire him, but I told him that after I beat him he can stay on in the job."

"You're very cocky, boy," Zack said.

"I learned that from you. Is that all you wanted to see me about? You're worried that I might lose my job?"

"That's right, but don't think it's because I'm worried about you. It just wouldn't do for the Tyler name to be embarrassed that way."

"Don't worry," the sheriff said, "I don't intend to besmirch the Tyler name."

"Just be sure you don't, boy, or you'll answer to me."

"Is that so?" Jack said. "You gonna get out of that bed and take me on?"

"Sonny, I don't have to get out of this bed to take you on. I can crush you right from here, and don't you forget it."

Jack Tyler laughed, but he did not turn his back until he was out in the hall.

Fran heard her brother coming back down the stairs and slipped into the kitchen to avoid him. However, at that moment Cliff Tyler came through the front door and ended up face to face with his older half brother.

"Well, well, brother Jack," Cliff said. "What brings you out here from town?"

"Official business," Sheriff Tyler replied.

"The old man sent for you, huh?"

Jack drew himself up to his full height, but still came two inches short on his younger half brother.

"The old man doesn't call for me, Cliff," he said. "That's your department. You're the one who works for him."

"Don't kid yourself, big brother," Cliff said. "We all work for him."

"Get out of my way, Mr. Foreman," Jack said.

"Oh, of course, *Sheriff*," Cliff said, stepping aside. "Anything you say."

As Jack stalked through the front door, Cliff laughed softly, shaking his head. He knew that he held the job Jack really wanted, running the Big T spread, but the old man had been smart enough to know who to give the badge to, and who to give the ranch to.

Cliff started up the stairs now, because it had already been fifteen minutes since the old man had sent for him, and Cliff knew that his father didn't like to be kept waiting.

Chapter Fifteen

That evening Clint Adams and Joe Bags met in the hotel dining room, and over dinner they talked about Bags's campaign.

"Speeches?" Bags asked.

"Of course you're going to have to make speeches, Bags," Clint said. "The people of Tylerville have to be told what your intentions are, what they can expect to gain by electing you instead of re-electing Jack Tyler."

"I never made a speech before."

"Don't worry about it. Just stand up and tell them why you want to be sheriff—and if that doesn't work, lie a little."

"Old Zack must know by now that I'm running against his son."

"I guess so."

"I wonder what his reaction was?"

"I think he sent for him," Clint said. "The sheriff's sister was in town today, looking for him. I get the feeling she's the old man's errand girl."

Bags wriggled his shoulders and said, "My back is starting to itch."

"I don't think you have to worry about that, yet," Clint said. "It's my opinion that the old man will try to buy you out first."

"Oh, yeah?" Bags asked. "I wonder how much I'm worth?"

"You'll just have to wait and find out," Clint said.

"What would you do?" Bags asked. "If it's a lot of money, I mean? What would you do?"

"I'd probably take it," Clint said.

"Ah," Bags said, "I'd probably just spend it real fast and be right back where I started from. I guess I'll just stay here and stick to my plan."

"Maybe you better wait and see how much is involved before you make that decision," Clint said.

"You really think it could be that much?" Bags asked.

"It's only my theory, Bags," Clint reminded him. "I think the old man's got so much money, he just naturally thinks it's his biggest weapon."

"I can't imagine what it must be like to be that rich," the deputy said.

"Neither can I."

Over coffee Bags asked, "You want to be my deputy when I win?"

"No."

"Just like that?"

"Just like that," Clint said. "After you win—or lose—I'll just be on my way. My days as a lawman are over."

"By choice?"

"Definitely."

"How old were you when you started?"

"A lot younger than you," Clint said.

"Don't want to talk about it, huh?"

"No."

"Okay."

After they'd paid the check Bags said, "What are you going to do now?"

"Go over to the saloon, I guess. Maybe find a poker game."

"You have any more dealings with Frank Bell?"

"No. I haven't seen him since that night."

"Well, watch out for him."

"I will."

Outside the hotel they split up, with Bags going on to do his rounds. Clint started for the saloon, but then changed his mind. It was Joe Bags's mention of Frank Bell that did it. It made him remember what Bags had said about Edie Bell, and that made him curious.

He changed his direction and walked over to the general store. He was sure he could find something to buy once he got there.

Chapter Sixteen

Edie Bell was a tall, statuesque brunette with large breasts, the brown, distended nipples of which were hovering only inches away from Clint Adams's face while she rode his rigid penis for all she was worth.

"Oh, God," she cried out, throwing her head back, revealing the long, graceful curve of her neck and throat. He could feel her insides clenching and unclenching on him, threatening to rip his orgasm right from him, and marveled at how quickly things had happened once he walked through the front door of the hardware store.

Frank Bell had been nowhere in sight, but Edie Bell had been standing behind the counter, and Clint had recognized her immediately from what Joe Bags had said—and from the look on Bags's face when he said it.

She was wearing a high-necked dress with buttons down the center, and her dark hair was swept up atop her head, showing off her long neck. Her breasts were prominent, to say the least, and she was tall enough to carry them well.

"Can I help you?" she asked in a husky voice.

"Uh, yes, I was looking for, uh—" and suddenly he couldn't think of anything to ask for.

"Me?" she asked then.

"What?"

"I asked if you were looking for me," she said, again.

"Uh, what would make you ask that?"

"Well," she said, putting her hands on her hips and thrusting her chest out, "you're obviously a stranger in town, and you've probably heard about me, so you wanted to come over and take a look."

"You think quite a lot of yourself, don't you?"

"Don't kid me, mister," she said. "It's happened before, that's all. They all come in here and try to figure out how they can get me around from behind this counter and back into that storeroom behind that curtain." She pointed out the curtain with a toss of her head.

"Many of them make it?" he asked.

"Not a one," she said, then added, "Yet." She sized him up some, and then asked, "You wouldn't be the fellow who took all of my husband's money in a poker game the other night, would you?"

"I would," he answered. "How'd you guess?"

"Didn't take no great brains," she said. "As far as I know, you're the only stranger in town, and he's been talking about you pretty steady since that night."

"We didn't hit it off."

"I'll say," she said. "But there's something else, too."

"What?"

"I think Frank's afraid of you."

"You do?"

"And I've never known him to be afraid of any man ever before. Were I you, I'd be extra careful."

"About what?"

"About Frank," she said. "If he is afraid of you, that's only gonna make him meaner and more dangerous. Why, if he ever came in here and found us talking together . . . and then if he could read my mind right now . . ."

"Why?" Clint asked. "What's on your mind?"

"Coming out from around this counter."

"And then what?"

"Well," she said, "if I did come out from behind this counter, I think the rest would be up to you."

"That sounds kind of like a challenge," Clint said.

"Maybe."

"It isn't much of a challenge, though," he went on, "if you aren't about to back it up by coming out from behind that counter."

"Now that," she said, "sounds like a challenge."

"It is."

"And are you ready to back it up?"

"You'll never know," he said, "staying behind that counter."

It was out in the open, now, and Clint knew he was taking an unnecessary risk. He knew that if Edie Bell came out from behind that counter, he wasn't about to walk away from her. He'd take her behind that curtain and into the storeroom and find a nice soft spot where he could plop her down on her back . . . and what about Frank Bell? What would happen if he came in at that point?

Things had gone too far to think about that.

She studied Clint for a few moments, then made her decision and strolled out from behind that counter. She approached him and came to within arm's reach. Her eyes were large and very blue, and her lips were very full—in fact, the upper lip was as full as the lower which gave her mouth a special, lush look.

"The next step is yours," she said.

He didn't hesitate. He took her by the arm and walked her through the curtain into the back room. Neither of them worried about the fact that the store was still open and anybody could have walked in—especially her husband.

They were too excited with each other, and by the situation, to care.

In the back room he suddenly grabbed her by both elbows and pulled her against him. His mouth covered hers and he savored those plush lips, pushing his tongue between them. She took his tongue between her teeth and chewed gently.

He pulled away from her then and looked around the room, then said, "There!" and steered her to a pile of grain sacks.

He undressed her quickly, as if afraid that she would change her mind, laid her clothes over the sacks and pushed her down on top. As she watched him he undressed himself and sank down on top of her, running his mouth over her breasts and nipples while she moaned and tangled her fingers in his hair.

Feverishly, they pressed against each other, as if each were trying to climb into the other's skin. Finally, she grabbed his stiff penis and guided it between her legs, where it sank in easily. He let out a moan as the heat and wetness of her engulfed him, and when he drove all the way in she answered with a moan of her own.

"On top," she whispered fiercely into his ear, "I want to be on top."

To oblige her he rolled over, remaining inside of her, so that she was sitting astride him. He reached around her and pulled her down so that he could suck on her nipples while she continued to ride him wildly. Burying his face in the valley between her breasts he slid his hands down her back until each was cupping one of her impressive globes.

"Oh, God," she said again, and when she drove down on him this time she stayed down, grinding herself down on him as her body was suddenly wracked by the tremors of her pleasure. When he felt her grip him tightly with her sheath he let himself go and spurted powerfully inside of her. She cried out and that was the first time Clint wondered if there was anyone in the store, listening to or watching what was going on.

The expression on Edie Bell's face said that she was way beyond any such thoughts. She had given herself up entirely to the moment, and when she opened her eyes they were cloudy.

"Edie," Clint said, trying to snap her out of it. Fun was fun, he thought then, but there was no point in pushing their luck.

"Mrs. Bell," he said, louder, and suddenly her eyes focused and she looked down at him.

"Oh, my God," she said. "What are we doing?"

"Something crazy," he said.

"But something wonderful," she said.

"True," he said, "but I still think we should get up and get dressed."

"Oh, yes, you're right," she said. She put her hands on his chest to push herself up, then impulsively leaned down to kiss him first, pressing those wonderfully full lips fleetingly against his.

"Let's get dressed," she said.

She got to her feet, and he followed, and they both rushed to get into their clothes, like two school kids who knew they had done something very wrong.

"How do I look?" she asked.

"Fine," he said. "Just fix your hair a little."

"Oh," she said, and started pushing loose tendrils of hair back into place.

"I think we'd better get outside," he suggested.

"All right," she said.

They walked to the curtains and she pulled them apart to walk through, then closed them again, quickly.

"What's wrong?" he asked.

"There's someone out there," she whispered.

"Your husband?"

She shook her head. "A customer. Mrs. Livingston."

He looked around, then went over to their passion place and picked up one of the grain sacks. "Let's go out. Just act natural, as if nothing was wrong."

"All right."

She took a deep breath, then parted the curtains and walked through, with Clint right behind her.

"Thank you for getting that sack yourself," she said. "I'm afraid I never would have been able to handle it."

"That's quite all right, Mrs. Bell," Clint said. "It was my pleasure."

"Hello, Mrs. Livingston," Edie Bell said, walking around behind the counter.

"Mrs. Bell," the spinsterish woman answered, giving Clint the fish eye.

"Thanks again, Mrs. Bell," Clint called from the door.

Edie Bell fixed her blue eyes right on Clint's and, with a smile that only he knew the meaning of, she said, "Oh, thank you . . ." and then realized that she didn't even know the man's name!

Clint walked out of the hardware store and started off down the street, wondering what the hell he was going to do with the sack of grain. He hefted it up onto his shoulder and started for the saloon.

He was going to have to tell Joe Bags that he had been so right about Mrs. Edie Bell. She was quite a woman, indeed.

As he was approaching the saloon he saw a buckboard parked outside a hardware store and, as he passed it, he dropped the sack of grain onto it, and continued onto the saloon for what he thought was a well deserved drink.

Chapter Seventeen

When Clint entered the saloon, he discovered why Frank Bell had not walked in on him and Edie Bell while they were looking for that sack of grain in the back room. Bell had already found a poker game and seemed to be doing very well for himself.

Clint walked to the bar and ordered a beer, then turned to watch the game. He was there almost ten minutes before Bell looked up and noticed him.

"Well, hello, friend," Bell called out, although it was clear by the look on his face that he did not regard Clint as a friend.

"Evening," Clint replied.

"Looks like we have a vacancy here, if you'd like to sit down and play," Bell said.

"No, thanks."

"Come on," Bell said. "Don't let this little pile of money in front of me scare you."

"It's not," Clint said.

"Well, it seems to me you ought to give a fella a chance to get back what money you took off of him."

"I don't see any of the other fellas I played with the other night at that table tonight," Clint said.

"I'm at this table," Bell pointed out.

Clint had been trying to spare the man embarrassment,

but Bell seemed intent on replaying the scene of the other night.

"I told you the other night, Bell, that I wouldn't play with you again," he reminded the man.

Bell's face flushed, and the other players were looking at each other impatiently. It was Bell's deal, and he was holding the game up.

"Come on, Frank, let's play the game," one of them said, and Bell gave the man a dirty look.

"You've got my money, friend," Bell said to Clint, "and I want you to sit down here and give me a chance to win it back."

"Sorry," Clint said, and turned his back on Bell, which angered the man even more. "Another beer," Clint said.

"Jesus, Frank, are we gonna play—" the man at the table said, and suddenly Bell stood up and stared down at the man, who was seated across the table from him.

"If you don't like the way I deal, Evans, you can sit out."

"I ain't even had a chance to see you deal, so I can't tell if I—" the man called Evans was saying, but he never got a chance to finish it. Bell leaned across the table and with his long reach was able to punch the man in the face, knocking him and his chair over backwards.

Bell shouted something then, and pushed the table aside while the other players scrambled to get out of the big man's way. He started after Evans, as if to take his anger out on him, but before he could reach him Clint Adams stepped between them.

"If you're mad at me, Bell, don't take it out on someone half your size."

Bell stopped short and stood up straight, eyeing the Gunsmith, whose name he still did not know.

"You're a pretty big man with that gun on your hip, ain't you?" Bell demanded. He himself was not carrying a gun.

"I don't need the gun, Bell," Clint said. "Not to take care of a big mouth like you."

Bell's face flushed a deeper red than it already was. "Am I supposed to believe that you won't go for that gun if I go for you?" he demanded.

"Only if you've got the nerve."

At that point Joe Bags walked into the saloon and took the situation in at one glance. He moved off to the side, away from the door, and leaned against the wall with his arms crossed to watch the proceedings.

"I'm gonna take you apart, friend," Bell said from between tightly clenched teeth.

"You're welcome to try," Clint said.

The man was tall, maybe six four, and he was wide and solid, with hands that were too large and clumsy for anything but hitting someone.

Bell was eyeing the Gunsmith carefully, wondering why a man who was smaller and lighter than he was not backing down from him. He could only assume that the man was egging him on, and would go for his gun when he made his move.

"Not while you're carrying that gun, mister," he said, finally. "I ain't nobody's fool. There'll be another time."

"You call it, friend," Clint said, standing easily with his hands at his sides. "It's up to you."

Bell glared at Clint, then turned, picked his money up off the floor—and if he picked up anybody else's they weren't man enough to claim it—and then left.

Clint turned and helped Evans to his feet.

"Thanks, mister," the man said. "He was gonna kill me."

"Have a drink on me," Clint said, "and forget it."

"Thanks."

Shakily Evans walked to the bar and ordered a shot of whiskey. Clint walked to another section of the bar, where his beer was waiting, and Bags pushed himself away from the wall and walked over next to him.

"Nice play," he said.

"Where were you when the law needed upholding?" Clint asked.

"I was watching," Bags assured him. "If he'd killed you I would have arrested him on the spot."

"That's comforting."

"Offer me a beer," Bags suggested.

"Buy your own."

"Don't get testy."

Bags ordered a beer, then said to Clint, "You're making it worse and worse."

"What?"

"Bell," Bags said. "You should have whipped him now and gotten over it."

"I always try and avoid trouble, Bags," Clint said. "You know that."

"Sure," Bags said. "That's how you earned your reputation."

"Are you going to start that shit again?" Clint asked.

"No, no, I'm not," Bags said. "Sorry I mentioned it."

"Drink your beer," Clint said. He felt foolish, almost fighting with a man whose wife he had just bedded, and he wasn't very proud of himself for either one of those things.

He wouldn't give back the latter, though. That was one of life's little occurrences that you thought back on fondly from time to time—but never repeated.

Still, if Edie Bell was willing, that was going to be one occurrence that would be hell not to repeat.

"You got something on your mind?" Bags asked.

"What?" Clint asked. "Oh, yeah, a couple of things. Nothing very important."

"As long as you're not mad at me for something."

"I'm not mad at anyone, Bags, except maybe myself. I think I'm just going to call it a night and turn in. I've got a picnic to go on tomorrow."

"Picnic? With who?"

"Fran Tyler."

"Fran Tyler!" Bags said. "I've been trying to catch her eye since I got to this town."

"Oh, I'm sorry," Clint said. "I really didn't mean to—"

"No, no, don't worry about me," Bags said. "You go and have your picnic and have a good time. There's plenty of women in town. Just watch out for her old man and her brothers."

"Half brothers," Clint said. "And she's really not close to any of them."

"She's a Tyler, Clint," Bags said. "And those people may not get along with each other, but they take that very seriously. Just follow my advice and watch your step."

"All right, pal," Clint said. "I'll watch it."

"And while you're at it," Bags said as Clint made for the door, "don't forget to watch mine, too."

Chapter Eighteen

Clint breakfasted alone the following morning, but spotted Joe Bags as soon as he left the hotel.

"Bags," he called out, and crossed the street to talk to him.

"Sleep okay?" Bags asked.

"Fine," Clint said. "I wanted to apologize to you for my mood last night."

"No reason," Bags said. "You went through a tense moment, not knowing whether or not you would have to kill a man."

Clint frowned and said, "You don't know me very well yet, do you?"

Bags looked at him, then replied, "You mean you wouldn't have used your gun if Bell charged you?"

"What do you think?"

"I think you'd have tried to take him on barehanded and gotten killed," Bags said. "That may seem right to you, but it seems awfully dumb to me, Clint."

"I'm not saying I would have let him kill me rather than use my gun," Clint said, "but I sure as hell would have tried a few other things first. Shooting somebody is not always the easiest answer, Bags."

"I guess neither one of us has changed all that much over the past few years," Bags said, frowning. He started to walk away, then turned around and said, "I hope when it comes to covering my back you won't feel the same way.''

Clint shook his head at that. ''If you've got doubts about me, you can get somebody else.''

''No. I can't think of anyone else I'd rather have—as long as you still want to stick around.''

''I do,'' Clint said.

''Okay, then,'' Bags said. ''I've got to go over to the newspaper office. Believe it or not, the editor of the Tylerville Gazette wants me to win. He's letting one of his copy boys make some signs for me. Want to come along?''

''I don't think so. You go ahead. I've got to make arrangements with the hotel for a picnic basket. And do me a favor, will you?'' Clint called out as Bags started away.

''What?'' Bags asked, turning around again.

''If you get word that Zack Tyler wants to see you, don't go without me.''

''If I can find you,'' Bags said.

''You can wait a few hours,'' Clint said. ''Remember, you asked me to hang around to cover your back, and you also asked me for advice. I'll give you the same advice you gave me. Watch out for the Tylers, and don't go and see any of them on your own.''

''You're a fine one to be giving that kind of advice,'' Bags said.

''What do you mean?''

''Well, who the hell are you going on a picnic with?''

''Bags.''

''What?''

''Go read your signs.''

Chapter Nineteen

Clint was looking forward to seeing much of the Big T spread, but he was to be disappointed. He had expected to pick Fran Tyler up at the house, but when he reached the gates he found the girl waiting there for him on horseback.

"Are you that anxious?" Clint asked her, but she wasn't listening. Her eyes were wide as she took in every inch of Duke.

"What an animal!" she finally said.

"Yeah," Clint said. "He's a good friend of mine."

"Do you own him?"

"Not really," Clint said. "We're more like partners."

"Can I ride him?" she asked, with a child's enthusiasm.

"That would be up to him," Clint said. "But if he didn't want you to you'd have to find out the hard way. I wouldn't advise it. Do you have someplace picked out for this picnic?"

"Oh, yes, I've got a spot in mind."

"Let's go then," he suggested, putting his arm over the basket behind him. "I'm anxious to get at this food."

"Follow me, then," she said. She was riding a roan and as she gigged him with her heels to get him started, Clint fell in line behind her.

After they rode that way for a few minutes she looked

back at him and said, "You know, you could ride next to me."

"Really?" he said. He rode up next to her and said, "I didn't want to take any liberties."

"Are you trying to tell me that you're a gentleman?"

"I like to think so," he said. "Why, can't you tell?"

"I don't really have anything to compare you with around here," she commented.

They rode on in silence for a few more minutes, and then he asked, "Why did you wait for me at the gate instead of letting me come up to the house?"

She hesitated a moment and then said, "I saved you the trouble of being looked over by my half brothers."

"Do they care that much who you see?"

"I'm a Tyler," she said, as if that answered the question.

"Anybody know you're coming out here with me?"

"No," she said. "I come and go as I please. I don't have to clear it with anyone . . . least of all any of my half brothers."

"What about your father?"

"I just tell him I'm going out, but make sure he knows I'll be back in time to give him his dinner."

"That's thoughtful."

She shrugged and said, "He's my father."

"Not by choice though, huh?"

Again she shrugged. "If we both had our way, I wouldn't be around here—only with him it would mean I was never born."

"And your way?"

"I'd just get out," she said, looking over at him. "If I had the nerve, I'd leave with a horse and the clothes on my back."

When he didn't ask, she supplied the answer anyway. "I don't have the nerve."

They didn't talk any more until they reached the picnic spot, a grassy knoll near a pond.

"Nice," Clint said as they dismounted.

"I come here sometimes," she said, "when I want to be alone."

"Ever bring anyone else here?"

She lowered her eyes to the ground and said, "No."

"I'm flattered."

She looked at him and said, "It's just a good spot for a picnic, that's all."

He pulled the basket down off of Duke's back. "So let's have a picnic."

He took a checkered tablecloth out of the basket, spread it on the ground, and then put the basket down. Together they started to unload the contents.

"Fried chicken," he said. "Baked potatoes—"

"Who's going to eat all this food?" she asked. "What's that?"

"That," he said, drawing it out, "is a fresh apple pie, and it cost me plenty."

"I love apple pie," she said, gleefully.

"Then it was worth it."

The presence of food—and good food, as it turned out—seemed to dispel any tension either of them might have felt, and they dug in, eating as if they were in a hurry to get to the apple pie.

"And now," Clint said, when they had finally reached that point. He reached into the basket for a knife to cut the pie with, and came up empty.

"What's wrong?" she asked.

"No knife," he said. "They didn't give me a knife to cut the pie with."

"Don't you have a knife?"

"I don't carry a knife," he said. "Only a gun—and you can't cut a pie with that."

"That sounds funny, coming from you," she said.

He stopped looking for the knife and looked at her. "Why?"

"Well, the way I heard it, you could do almost anything with a gun."

"Where did you hear that?"

She shrugged and said, "I heard it."

"Would you like me to add to my reputation by pulling my gun and shooting the pie into pieces?"

"No, that's not what I meant," she said. "You're sensitive about that, aren't you? I mean, about your reputation."

"Yeah, I'm sensitive."

"Yes," she said, reaching over to touch his face, "I can see that you are."

"Does that surprise you?"

"Yes," she admitted, frankly.

"That's why I'm sensitive—touchy—about my reputation," he told her. "That's why I don't like it."

"I guess I never thought of a man with a reputation not liking it," she said. "I always thought that men wanted reputations. My father has a reputation as a mean, vicious businessman, and he loves it."

"Some men do like it," Clint admitted. "I don't think Bill Hickok ever minded it. In fact, he built it himself, but in the end it got him killed.

"Did you know Wild Bill Hickok?"

"Yeah," Clint said, "he was a friend of mine, a very good friend of mine."

"I'm sorry," she said. "I'm sorry I made a dumb remark without thinking."

"That's okay," he said. "Now what do you say we find a way to eat this pie?"

"I know a way," she said suddenly.

"Yeah?"

"Yeah."

She drove her hand into the pie, picked up a handful and held it out to him. He started laughing, and before long they were both laughing, faces covered with apple pie, and once again the tension between them was broken.

Chapter Twenty

"How about a swim?" Fran asked after they had digested the pie—the entire pie, split equally between them.

"I don't have anything to wear," he protested.

"I'm game if you are," she said. "Or are you shy?"

"I've never been accused of that," he said, "but are you sure—"

"I'm very sure," she said, looking at him right in the eye.

With that she stood up and began to unbutton her blouse. Clint, determined not to watch, stood up and busied himself with his own clothes, while very conscious of the sound her clothing was making as it slid off her body.

"Here I go," she said.

He looked up just in time to see her dive into the pond, the sun reflecting off her pale, taut buttocks. In moments he too was naked, and followed her into the pond.

The water was cold, a pleasant contrast to the mildness of the day, and he felt goose bumps threatening to cover his body. When he surfaced he shook his head to clear the water from his eyes and started looking for Fran.

"Here," she shouted, waving to him from about twenty feet away. She was bobbing in the water, and as she waved to him her breasts rose out of the water and were in clear view. They too were pale, as firm looking as her buttocks, with the nipples swelling in response to the coldness of the water.

"Try and catch me," she called, and began to swim away from him.

She was an excellent swimmer and it took him some time to finally catch up to her. When he did he grabbed for her, but his hands slid off her slippery flesh. Finally, he wrapped his arms around her and mashed her breasts against his chest.

"Is this what you wanted?" he asked.

She looked into his eyes and said, "Yes."

He kissed her and they sank beneath the surface, breathing from each other's mouths. He slid his mouth free and moved to her breasts, sucking on her nipples while they were still under water.

When they broke the surface together he said, "I think we'd better go to dry land and do this right—unless you want to drown."

"I'll race you," she said, and started off.

He caught her just before they reached the bank and lifted her up to carry her out of the water. She nestled into his arms and began running her lips over his neck while he carried her to their picnic spot and laid her on the tablecloth.

He kissed her again and began running his hands over her body. She moaned into his mouth and reached between them, wrapping both hands around his erection.

They took turns becoming acquainted with each other's body while the sun dried them in time for their bodies to become moist with perspiration; then he found her moist, deep channel and filled it. She groaned as he entered her and wrapped her legs around him, surprising him with her powerful thighs.

"Oh, yes, Clint, yes," she cried out, and there was no one around for miles to hear as her cries rose and became screams. He reached beneath her to cup her buttocks in his hands and continued to take her in long, deep strokes, until finally both of their bodies achieved that final convulsion of pleasure, together.

After they had dressed and packed up everything, Clint secured the basket to the back of his saddle, then turned to face Fran.

"We should do this again sometime," he said.

"And soon," she agreed. Laughing, she threw her arms around him and kissed him hard, rubbing her body against him.

"Not this soon," he said, slapping her on the rump.

"Why not?"

"Because I'm a lot older than you, that's why," he said.

"Bullspit."

"Fran Tyler, you shock me."

"Well, to tell you the truth," she admitted, "I shocked myself today, too."

"Sorry?"

"Not at all."

"I guess we'd better get back to what we're both supposed to be doing," he said.

"What's that?" she asked, and then quickly said, "No, don't tell me."

"Why not?"

"Because that's what Sheriff Jack wants," she said.

"What are you talking about?"

"Jack wanted me to find out what you were doing in town."

"Is that why you came on the picnic?" he asked.

"No," she answered quickly. "I told him to go to hell. I came on this picnic because I wanted to, and for no other reason. You got to believe that, Clint."

"I do," he said, putting his arms around her and pulling her close. "I believe you, Fran."

"So I don't want you telling me why you came to Tylerville, you hear?"

"Hell, I don't mind telling you that," he said, releasing her so he could look at her face. "I'm just passing through, Fran, and that's the truth. I had nothing else in mind when I came to Tylerville, and that's the truth."

"I believe you, Clint."

Of course, Clint thought, *once I got here things changed a little*. But still, he had told her the truth. There was no reason for her to know that he was watching Joe Bags's back while he ran against her brother for the sheriff's job.

"Let's mount up," he said.

"Hell," she said then, grinning, "I thought that was what you just did."

"Little lady," Clint said, climbing up on Duke's back, "you're getting more shocking by the minute."

Chapter Twenty-One

This time she didn't even let him get near the front gates of the ranch.

"When will I see you again?" she called out as he started away.

"That's up to you," he replied, and kept going.

When he got back to town the sheriff was out on the street; Clint tipped his hat. Sheriff Tyler watched the Gunsmith ride to the livery, and then went back into his office. He had not missed seeing the picnic basket on the back of Clint's saddle.

Clint put Duke up at the livery, then went back to the hotel and returned his basket, while giving his compliments to the cook. After that, he went to the saloon for a drink, which was the only thing he hadn't brought with him in the picnic basket.

When Clint walked into the saloon he was surprised to see a sign on the wall that said "Joe Bags for Sheriff"— especially in a saloon owned by Zack Tyler.

"Isn't that a little chancy?" he asked the bartender.

The barkeep shrugged and said, "I didn't put it up, the deputy did. It's his problem when Tyler sees it."

"Yeah, I guess it is," Clint said. He leaned his elbows on the bar and said, "You wouldn't be thinking about bringing it to his attention, would you?"

The bartender shook his head and said, "He'll see it soon enough on his own. Can I get you something?"

"A beer," Clint said. "A cold one."

"Comin' up."

Clint wondered where else Bags had hung those signs, and what he'd been thinking about when he hung that one here, in Tyler's own saloon.

"Here you go," the bartender said, setting down the beer.

"Thanks."

It was the bartender's turn to lean on the bar. "Are you and the deputy friends?"

Clint looked at the man and said, "You might say that. Why?"

"Strikes me he's going to need all the friends he can get, running against Tyler in this town."

"So?"

"I was just wondering if you were planning on backing his play."

Clint took a good look at the bartender. The man was tall and thin, in his mid-thirties, and all of a sudden he was asking too many questions.

"Why do you ask?"

"Oh, uh, just curious."

"You sure Tyler didn't put the idea in your head?"

The bartender made a face, said, "Which one?" and then went down the bar to clean an imaginary wet spot.

As if on cue, Jack Tyler walked into the saloon just then, and Clint watched his face for his reaction to the sign.

The sheriff smiled, and then laughed out loud.

"He's really serious," he said aloud, to no one in particular. The other customers in the saloon looked up at him, but quickly went about their own business.

Tyler walked up to the bar and stood next to Clint.

"Sheriff," Clint said, by way of greeting.

"Adams," Tyler replied. He held up a finger to the bartender, who reacted instantly. "Enjoying your stay in Tylerville?"

"Very much," Clint replied.

"Yes," the lawman said, accepting a beer from the bartender, "I noticed. I saw you ride in a little while ago, with a picnic basket."

"That's right," Clint said. "It was a beautiful day for a picnic."

"I hope you had good company for it," Tyler said.

"Oh, I did, Sheriff," Clint said. "It's real nice of you to be concerned."

"Just want you to enjoy your stay in my town."

"Well, you don't have to worry about that," Clint assured him. "I'm enjoying it just fine."

"Good, good," Tyler said.

Clint looked at the sign Bags had put up, and then back at Sheriff Tyler.

"Looks like you have some competition for your job."

"You mean that?" Tyler said, turning around and leaning his elbows on the bar. He looked at the sign and said, "That's no competition, believe me. This town knows who its sheriff should be. They won't have any problem making a choice."

"I understand this saloon is owned by your . . . family," Clint commented. He had almost said "by your father" but had changed his mind at the last moment. As it turned out, he needn't have bothered.

"My father owns this saloon, Adams," Tyler said. "Everybody knows that."

"Do you think he'd like the idea of that sign being in here?" Clint asked.

"I think once I explain it to him, he won't mind at all," Tyler said. "See, my deputy has the right to try his best to get elected. If my father or I tried to stop him, all we'd be doing is helping him. Do you understand?"

"Oh, I understand, Sheriff," Clint said. "I just don't recall hearing that your father had a reputation for fair play."

"Well, you of all people should know how misleading reputations can be, Adams."

Clint stared at Jack Tyler, and then said, "Yes, I suppose you have a point, Sheriff."

Tyler sipped his beer and then asked, "Do you think you'll be in town long enough to see the results of the election?"

"Well, I don't know. That's a couple of weeks away, at least."

"Aren't you interested in how your friend will do?"

"I'm sure Bags will make a good showing for himself," Clint said, "as long as he is allowed to."

"Well, why shouldn't he be?" Jack asked. "It'll be a good lesson for him when he loses. He'll learn something."

"Yeah, I'm sure he will," Clint agreed. "I'm sure he will."

Chapter Twenty-Two

The offer to Joe Bags was made the next day, by Mayor Tidyman, on behalf of Zack Tyler—although Bags wasn't told that.

The deputy was performing rounds when he got word that the mayor wanted to see him. Bags figured it had something to do with his candidacy—and he was right.

"You wanted to see me, Mr. Mayor?" Bags asked.

At that point Tidyman was more sorry than ever that he was beneath Zack Tyler's thumb. Sheriff Jack Tyler never called him "Mr. Mayor," and neither did old Zack. It would be nice to hear from a man wearing the sheriff's star. . . .

"Have a seat, Deputy," Tidyman said. "I have something to discuss with you."

Bags removed his hat and sat in the chair directly in front of the mayor's desk.

"What's it about?" Bags asked.

"It's about you running for sheriff," Tidyman said. "Deputy, do you think that Jack Tyler is a good sheriff?"

"As good as some, worse than others," Bags replied, wondering what this was all about.

"A lot of people in this town think he's better than most," the mayor said.

"They'll get their chance to vote," Bags said.

"Yes, of course," Tidyman said, "but there are some

people who, uh, would prefer that a vote wasn't necessary."

Bags was starting to get a glimmer of what this was about, and he was surprised—although he guessed he shouldn't have been. Zack Tyler owned the town; it stood to reason that he would also own the mayor.

"What do you mean?"

Tidyman shifted uncomfortably in his chair. "There are some people would prefer that there wasn't an election and would be willing to, ah—*compensate* you for withdrawing from the election."

"I see," Bags said.

"Ah, I thought you might," Tidyman said, happily.

"How much compensation are we talking about here, Mr. Mayor?" Bags asked.

"Uh, well, quite a bit," Tidyman said. "I imagine it would take quite a bit to soften the, uh, blow of not running for sheriff."

"If I ran I'd probably win," Bags said. "Is that what these 'people' are afraid of?"

"No, of course not," Tidyman said. "He's—uh, they're just concerned with avoiding ah, uh, unnecessary process—"

"Mr. Mayor," Joe Bags said, standing up, "you tell Zack Tyler that if he has an offer to make to me he better make it in person. I don't talk to middlemen. Good day."

"Uh, Deputy," Tidyman said, coming out of his chair, "I didn't say anything about Mr. Tyler—"

"I know you didn't," Bags said, "and you don't have to worry. I'll tell him you didn't mention his name until I did."

"Uh, well, I thank you—uh, I mean—"

When Bags left the office the mayor was fishing out a handkerchief to wipe the perspiration from his brow. Suddenly, it had gotten very hot in his office.

•   •   •

Bags found Clint working in his rig and told him about the offer Mayor Tidyman had made.

"That figures," Clint said, "although I hadn't thought of it, either. What did you tell him?"

"I told him that if Zack Tyler had an offer to make me, let him make it in person."

"Why didn't you just turn him down?"

"I want to see Zack Tyler's face when I do that," Bags said.

"You're playing this dangerously, Bags," Clint warned him.

"It got dangerous as soon as I made the announcement that I was running," Bags said. "Do you think that the sheriff knows about his old man's offer?"

"I don't know," Clint said, "but there is one way to find out."

"Go and ask him?"

Clint shook his head. "Mention the offer that came from the mayor, and say that you wonder who could be behind it. Let the sheriff draw his own conclusions. Maybe if you get the two of them fighting each other, you won't have to worry about either of them."

"You've got a devious mind, Clint Adams," Bags said, admiringly.

"It comes with experience, Bags."

Chapter Twenty-Three

Clint and Bags both decided to just go over to the saloon, sit in a corner and nurse some beers until Sheriff Jack Tyler walked in. It was a good bet that Tyler would approach them, just to make a few remarks to his deputy and rival for the sheriff's job.

"Should we play cards, or something?" Bags asked between beers.

"Just the two of us?" Clint asked.

"Well, I'm sure we could round up a couple of more players," Bags said.

"Might cost you some votes," Clint said.

"Why?" Bags asked. "Playing cards with some of the townspeople might win me some votes."

"Not if you beat them."

"I see your point," Bags said, taking a sip from his beer.

"And nurse that beer," Clint said.

"Why?"

"I think you should keep your eyes clear for the next couple of weeks," Clint advised him. "You want to know everything that's going on around you—especially if you become sheriff."

"I can drink a half a dozen of these without feeling a thing," Bags argued.

Clint stared at him and said, "That's what I'm afraid of."

Bags didn't quite understand what that meant, but he lifted the beer to his lips, then thought better of it, put it down on the table and stared at it as if it were a cup of hemlock.

Clint was about to get up and get a deck of cards from the bartender, to while away the time with solitaire, when the batwing doors opened to admit two men. The Gunsmith's sixth sense began to tingle and he sat back down again.

"What's the matter?" Bags asked.

"The two men who just walked in," Clint said.

Bags looked up at them, and then asked, "What about them?"

"I don't know," Clint said, still watching the men as they advanced on the bar. "They don't feel right."

"They look all right to me," Bags said.

"Just the same, let's watch them for a while," Clint said.

Bags started fiddling with his beer glass, which was almost empty, while Clint watched the two men closely. They both stood with their back to the room, but Clint clearly saw each man look into the mirror twice, possibly at the table he and Bags were seated at.

Impatiently, Bags said, "I'm going to get that deck of cards," and started to get up.

"Wait—" Clint said.

"Or a beer, or something," Bags said, thinking that Clint was objecting to the cards.

Bags strode to the bar, and as Clint started to rise, sensing something, he knew that he wasn't rising fast enough.

One of the men drew his gun with enough speed to impress even the Gunsmith and shoved the barrel into Joe Bags's ribs. The other man turned and drew his gun in a much more leisurely fashion and pointed it at Clint.

"What's the play?" Clint demanded from the two men. He was in a crouch, halfway between standing and sitting, and had not drawn his gun for fear of Bags's safety.

"Just sit back down, Mr. Gunsmith," the man facing him said, "and put your gun on the table, or my friend there will put a hole in *your* friend. Understand?"

"I understand," Clint said.

He sat back down and slowly took out his gun and placed it on top of the table.

"Now I'm gonna walk over there and pick it up," the man said, "and if you should try something funny like turning the table over—"

"I'm not going to try anything," Clint said, cutting him off.

"Well, good," the man said.

He came forward carefully, reached for the Gunsmith's weapon and tucked it into his gunbelt.

"Now the deputy's gun, Lem," the man said to his friend.

"I got it already," the man called Lem said, touching Bags's gun, which was already tucked into his gunbelt. "Now what?"

"Now a friend of yours wants to talk to you," the first man said, backing away. He backed all the way to the batwing doors and called out, "You can come in now."

No one else in the saloon had moved since the two men had drawn their guns, but now all eyes moved to the doors to see who was going to walk in.

Frank Bell came walking into the saloon, looking as massive as ever. He fixed the Gunsmith with a glassy stare and said, "Now let's see how tough you are without your gun."

Chapter Twenty-Four

"I don't believe it," Joe Bags said, staring at Frank Bell, who was more than a little drunk.

"Shut up, Deputy," the man called Lem said, reinforcing his words by jabbing Bags in the stomach with his gun. Bell, however, hadn't seemed to hear Bags's words. In fact, he didn't see or hear anything, as he was concentrating totally on Clint Adams.

"Stand up, Adams," he said.

Everyone else in the saloon was looking at each other, and then at the two men with the guns, wondering if they should stay where they were, or try to get up and out of there.

"What about these other people, Bell?" Clint said. "They'll only get in our way."

Bell didn't seem to hear the words at first, then shook his head a bit, as if to clear it, and said, "Everybody out—except the deputy."

And, naturally, his two gunmen.

Bell continued to glare at Clint while the other people filed out of the saloon, and there was so much malevolence in the man's eyes that Clint had to wonder if he didn't know about the session in the back room with Edie Bell.

Could she have told him?

"All right," Bell said. "The other people are gone.

Come out from around that table, Mr. Gunsmith, and let's see what kind of a man you are without your gun.''

''Remember Mexico,'' Joe Bags said, reminding Clint of the last time he had seen him take on a bigger man. Clint had won that time, but just barely.

Could he get lucky twice?

Clint came around from behind the table, feeling very light on the right side, where his gun normally was. There was a distinct possibility that he was about to absorb a severe beating at the hands of Frank Bell, but the thing that was uppermost in his mind was the worry that he might not be able to get that modified Colt out from his back when it was all over.

Sizing Frank Bell up, the Gunsmith tried to analyze his own advantages. He was lighter and probably faster, but he knew he could not match Bell for strength. He had to stay out of reach of those powerful arms. The only other advantage was the fact that Bell was obviously drunk. Though you couldn't tell from his movements, Clint could see it in his eyes, and if the fight went on long enough, it might end up having some bearing on the outcome.

''Come on,'' Bell told Clint, waving him to him. Both of the armed men were now standing on either side of Joe Bags, who had been allowed to turn around and watch.

''I'm here, Bell,'' Clint said. ''Come and get me—if you can.''

Bell seemed to pause to think about that, and then came shambling forward slowly, instead of charging as Clint had hoped. The Gunsmith had originally planned to side-step the big man's charge and trip him up, but with Bell coming forward very deliberately, he had to change his tactics.

Clint began to back away as Bell advanced, then stopped as he realized his back would soon be against the wall.

''Keep backing away, Adams,'' Bell taunted him. ''Back right up to the wall, so I can put you through it.''

Just as Bell finished talking, Clint stepped in and quickly threw two left jabs into the man's face. They surprised Bell, but had little more effect than that.

"Gotta do better than that," Bell said.

Again, as Bell finished talking Clint stepped in, and this time he threw two hard rights. Bell's upper lip split, but he tasted his own blood and smiled, showing blood-smeared teeth. He had learned something, though, and this time he didn't speak.

Trying a new tack, Clint faked a move to his left, and when Bell took a step to his left, Clint moved to the right and threw a kick at Bell's stomach. Bell, quick for a big man, caught the Gunsmith's foot and twisted, throwing Clint off balance and sending him crashing to the floor. Having accomplished that, Bell got a little wild and tried to stomp Clint, who rolled away, far enough to be able to scramble back to his feet.

Grinning through the blood that was leaking from his upper lip, Bell continued to stalk Clint, who had new respect for the man's speed, even under the influence of alcohol.

Clint tried stepping in and out and peppering the man's face with rights and lefts, but they seemed to do nothing but smear the lower portion of his face with blood. Clint had a feeling that Frank Bell's face had been anesthetized by the alcohol he'd consumed.

Clint had to strike at an area where Bell would feel the blow.

He tried maneuvering around Bell, but the man would step quickly right and left to cut him off. Clint once again faked to his left, and when Bell moved that way, the Gunsmith launched a kick at his opponent's groin. Bell turned so as to take the blow on his big thigh, and when he did Clint stepped off to his right and threw another kick, this time to Bell's exposed left kidney area. When his boot exploded on Bell's kidney, the man's mouth dropped open and his eyes popped. Completing the move, Clint stepped behind Bell and, using all of his weight, propelled him into the wall, where he struck shoulder first.

Clint took a quick glance at the bar, where the three men were watching the fight, before picking up a chair and advancing towards the crouched Bell. He raised it up as if to strike Bell with it, then whirled quickly and threw the chair towards the three spectators. He threw it high, deliberately missing them, but as he'd hoped, they ducked, expecting the chair to come towards them. Clint had been hoping that Bags would stay alert, and the deputy rewarded him. Although he too had ducked the chair, he recovered first and threw an elbow into Lem's face, connecting solidly with a cheekbone, which gave way. Next, he clamped his hand over the wrist of the other man's gunhand, pinned it to the man's chest and then brought a knee up into the midsection, doubling his man over. With a wrench of his hand on the man's wrist, he disarmed him, while pulling Clint's gun from the man's belt.

At the other end of the floor, Clint suddenly realized that he was paying too much attention to what was happening at the bar, and when he turned back to Bell he realized that he was too late.

Frank Bell came springing off the wall with his powerful arms spread wide and wrapped them around the Gunsmith. Turning back to the wall, Bell rammed Clint into it, driving the breath from his body and slamming the back of his head off the wall.

As Bell's arms tightened around him, restricting his breathing, Clint started seeing flashing lights and darkness. Through it he heard two quick shots, then silence broken only by the ringing in his ears, and then, as the darkness enveloped him totally, one last shot and a flash of pain in his side. . . .

Chapter Twenty-Five

Coming back was like swimming through mud, but when Clint finally made it he saw the face of Edie Bell.

"He's awake," she said to someone out of his eyesight. He moved his head to see who she was talking to, but lights flashed before his eyes and he cut the movement short.

"How do you feel?" someone asked him.

He thought about the question for a few moments, then decided that it was stupid and he wouldn't answer it—at least, not until he knew who was asking it.

"Who wants to know?"

"Well, at least you can talk," the man's voice said. "That's more than we got the other three times you woke up."

"Who—"

"All right, relax," the voice said. "I'll tell you who I am and where you are—"

"I know where I am, damn it," Clint said, irritably. He was in his own hotel room. He recognized it from the peeling ceiling above his bed.

"All right, relax," the voice said. Clint took a chance on moving his eyes and located the man's face without any pain. I'm Dr. Madonna," the man said. "Michael Madonna."

"Glad to meet you," Clint said. "Am I in one piece?"

''As far as I can tell.''

''I heard shots,'' Clint said, ''felt a pain in my side . . .''

''That doesn't necessarily add up to your being shot,'' the doctor said.

''Well then tell me what it does add up to.''

''The pain you felt in your side was from a broken rib, which was caused by Frank Bell's incredible strength.''

''He had his arms wrapped around me—''

''And he doesn't even like you,'' Madonna said, ''or so I have to assume.''

The doctor obviously fancied himself something of a comedian, but the Gunsmith wasn't laughing. For one thing, as soon as Madonna had mentioned his rib, he became aware of the pain in his side, which increased every time he took a breath. He also became aware of the fact that his upper torso was wrapped tight.

''I can't breathe,'' he said. ''You've got me wrapped up too tight.''

''You've got a cracked rib, friend,'' the doctor said. ''If you want it to separate and puncture your side, then we'll unwrap you. It's your decision.''

It was an easy one. ''I think I'll . . . keep it wrapped . . . for a while,'' Clint said through the pain.

''It'll hurt less if you don't talk, and breathe as shallowly as you can.'' Packing up his black bag the doctor said, ''Mrs. Bell has agreed to stay with you and notify me if anything goes wrong.''

''What could go wrong?''

''A few things,'' the doctor answered, ''but don't worry about it. I'll do the worrying.'' Ready to go, he picked up his bag and spoke once more to Clint. ''The sheriff wants to talk to you, and so does your friend, the deputy. I told them I'll let them know when I think you're ready—and that won't be today. I'll see you tomorrow.''

''Doc—''

''Don't talk, friend. It's going to hurt like the devil

anyway, but the less you talk, the less it'll hurt.''

"I'll keep him quiet, Doctor," Edie Bell said.

The doctor nodded, put on his hat and left.

"What happened?" Clint asked.

"Quiet."

"Tell me."

"I don't know, I wasn't there," she said. "All I know is you got hurt, and Frank got shot."

"Is he dead?"

"I hope so," she said, with feeling.

"Get me Bags," Clint said.

"You're supposed to keep quiet."

"Get me Bags and then I'll keep quiet."

"Promise?"

"I promise."

She frowned at him, then said, "Oh, all right. I'll be right back."

As she walked out the door, Clint made the mistake of closing his eyes. When he woke up it was eight hours later, but Bags was there.

"You wanted to see me?" he asked when he saw that Clint was awake.

"Yeah," Clint said, frowning. "I must have dozed off."

"Sure, for eight hours."

"Eight hours!"

"Relax, you needed the rest."

"Ask him what you wanted to ask him so he'll leave," Edie told Clint. "He's supposed to keep quiet," she said to Bags.

"So are women," Bags said, "but that never stopped any of you."

They glared at each other for a few minutes and then Clint cleared his throat. "Remember me?"

"I guess you want to know what happened after you went under," Bags said.

"Exactly. I heard two shots as I was going out, and then

a third. Who got shot, who did the shooting?''

''I disarmed Bell's two friends and when I looked at you, you were pinned to the wall. Then, when Bell picked you up in his arms and started squeezing, Tyler came barging through the doors with his gun out.''

''I guess I owe him my life then, huh?''

''Like hell!'' Bags spat. ''He fired two shots into the ceiling, and when I saw that was it, I pumped one into Bell myself . . . with your gun!'' he finished with a big grin.

Clint stared at him for a few heartbeats, and then said, ''So you finally got to fire my gun.''

''Yep,'' Bags said, ''and she shoots sweet. Got him right where I wanted to.''

''Kill him?''

''Not unless the bullet traveled.''

''Where'd you shoot him?''

''Right where he sits.''

Chapter Twenty-Six

It was three days before the Gunsmith even felt strong enough to try and get up, and even then it was against the advice of the doctor.

"It's a foolish move," he told Clint, "but it's your body."

"That's right," Clint said, "and it's getting out of this bed today, before it takes root."

"I won't take the responsibility—"

"No, but I will," Clint said. "I appreciate what you've done, Doc, but if you're going to be critical, you can leave."

"Very well," Madonna said, "then I will. He's all yours, Mrs. Bell."

As the doctor went out, Edie said under her breath, "Don't I wish."

"What?" Clint said.

"Nothing. Are you going to insist on this madness?" she asked.

"Yes," he said, "and if you're not going to help—"

"I'll help, I'll help," she said.

"Then get me my pants," he said.

"Before I get your pants," she suggested, "why don't you see if you can stand?"

"I can stand," Clint said. He threw the covers aside, winced at the slight pain it caused him. The day before he

103

had noticed that he'd started breathing a bit easier, with less pain—or maybe he was just getting used to the pain. Whatever it was, though, he was feeling better—slightly—and wanted to get out of bed.

Bags had been to see him each day, and told him that Zack Tyler had made no attempt to talk to him, or to kill him.

But there was no telling how long that would continue—especially the latter.

So, he had to get up and keep an eye on Bags's back. The closer it got to the election, the larger a target it became.

"Do you want help?" Edie asked.

"I can get up," he insisted.

Gritting his teeth he swung his legs to the floor, and found that the pain was not too bad. The back of his head had stopped hurting altogether, unless he probed it, and he no longer had a headache. If he could stand up without causing tremendous pain to his rib, he'd be home free.

"Careful," she said as she saw him preparing to stand.

"I can do it," he said again.

Only the fact that Edie was a large woman enabled her to catch him when he fell and keep him from hitting the floor.

"Damn!" he snapped, lying in her arms like a baby.

"Let's get you back to bed," she said.

"I can do it!" he insisted.

"All right," she said, "but let's do it tomorrow."

It was another two days before he tried again, and this time he was sure he could do it, because of what had happened the night before. . . .

"You want to try again tomorrow?" she had asked him.

"Yes."

"Then let's test you tonight," she proposed.

"How?" he asked, frowning.

"Like this," she said, approaching the bed and getting on her knees. He watched as she removed the covers from him, then ran her hand over his crotch through his underwear. Immediately, his penis responded and began to swell.

"I've been wanting to touch you for days," she said, "and I've been holding back. I can't hold back any longer If you can survive this without much pain, " she said, continuing to knead him through his shorts, "then we'll let you get up. All right?"

"Do I have a choice?" he asked.

"No," she said, removing his shorts. "No choice at all."

She grasped his erection in both hands and, leaning over him, licked the swollen head. Sliding both hands down to the base she began to lave his rod with her tongue, up and down, flicking the tip playfully, and then finally taking it into her mouth. He took a breath as she swallowed him up and hardly felt the pain. The sensations that she was causing were overpowering.

"God, Edie . . ." he said, running his fingers through her hair.

She moaned with her mouth full, and then her head began to bob up and down while she curled her fingers around the base of his cock. She slid the length of him in and out of her mouth, never quite allowing the head to pop free. His tip began to leak a milky fluid, and the taste inflamed her desire even more. Moaning, she gripped the base of his shaft with her fingers and quickened the motions of her head, sucking at the same time, and suddenly his seed was spewing forth into her mouth and she was swallowing it all, desperate to capture every drop. The pain in his side was nothing compared to the exquisite pain and pleasure caused by her mouth and hands.

The next day, he got to his feet with almost no problem.

Chapter Twenty-Seven

Strapping on his gun, Clint ignored Edie Bell's continuous protestation and glanced out the window at the street below. He hadn't been outside for five days, and he was starting to go slightly stir crazy.

"Where's my hat?" he asked, right in the middle of one of Edie's sentences.

"You're not even listening to me, are you?" she demanded.

"No," he answered truthfully. "Where's my hat?"

"On the chair in the corner."

He walked over to get it and jammed it down on his head.

"This is crazy, Clint,"

"No, it's not," he said. "You made the deal last night, now stick to it."

"Let me walk with you, then. You can lean on—"

"I'm not going to lean on anyone, Edie," he said. "You better go back to your store—and don't think I don't appreciate everything you've done for me."

"Sure," she said. She picked up her wrap and started for the door.

"What about Frank, Edie?" he asked.

"He's in jail," she answered. "Doc took care of him and he'll spend some more time in jail. I guess the sheriff will want to see if you want to press charges."

"What about the other two men?"

"I don't know anything about them," she said, glumly.

Clint watched her leave without speaking to her further. When she was gone he stood in the center of the room, closed his eyes and took an experimental breath. The ache in his rib was still there, but it was bearable.

He left his hotel room, took the stairs slowly, and then headed for the sheriff's office.

When he entered the office Jack Tyler looked up from his desk and raised his eyebrows in surprise.

"Well, look who's up and out," he said.

"I understand you've been wanting to talk to me," Clint said, trying to walk naturally across the room. He did not try to sit, because he would not have been able to do that with natural ease.

"Sure did, but that fool doctor wouldn't let anyone near you," Tyler said. Apparently he didn't know that Clint had talked with Joe Bags. "Nobody but Edie Bell, that is," Tyler added with a glint in his eyes, "and with her husband in my jail, too."

"How is he?" Clint asked.

"He'll live, he just won't be sitting for a while."

"No thanks to you, I understand," Clint said.

Tyler frowned and said, "Bags fired before me, that's all."

"You fired in the air," Clint reminded him.

"I ain't about to shoot a man in the back without first giving him some kind of warning," Tyler said.

"Guess you didn't think of shooting him in the butt."

"I guess not," Tyler said.

"What about the other two?" Clint asked. "The men with the guns?"

"Ran them out of town."

"Why not jail them?"

"For what? Bell was the one behind the whole thing. Those men were only doing what they were paid to do."

"I see," Clint said. "That makes it okay."

"Man's gotta make a living."

"Sure, " Clint said. "You got any kind of beef with me?"

"No," Tyler answered. "The other two men explained the whole story to me. Bell had it in for you, but didn't want to go up against you while you were wearing your gun, so he hired those two to get it off of you—which they did pretty easily, I understand."

Clint didn't comment.

"Anyway, they told the story straight, so I've got no beef with you, as long as your story is the same."

Clint told Tyler what happened, and the sheriff kept nodding his head.

"Yep, that's the way they told it. Guess you were pretty lucky to come out of this thing alive."

"Thanks to Bags."

"Looks like I'm lucky you don't live in this town," Tyler said. "You sound like you'd vote for my deputy."

"I would if I could, Tyler," Clint said, moving towards the door, "but there are quite a few people in this town who *can* and will—and that might make a difference."

Chapter Twenty-Eight

When Clint left Tyler's office he went looking for Joe Bags. He passed the doctor on the way, who said nothing, but stared after the Gunsmith, shaking his head.

Clint went to the saloon, ordered a beer and asked the bartender if he'd seen Bags.

"Not today," the man said. "You're back on your feet a lot sooner than people expected."

"That's why I'm back on my feet," Clint said. He looked around and saw that the sign that had been promoting Bags for sheriff had been taken down, and one for Tyler had been substituted.

"What happened to the sign?"

"Tyler came in the morning after the fight and switched them," the bartender answered.

"Maybe he's worried," Clint said.

"Maybe."

The man went off to serve another customer and Clint drank his beer standing straight up, wishing he could lean on the bar.

He hoped Bags hadn't been foolish enough to go out to the Big T spread and see Zack Tyler all alone, but if he hadn't gone there, then where the hell was he?

Clint decided to take the beer to a table and lowered himself gingerly into a chair. Getting off his feet relieved some of the pressure he'd been feeling in his side, and he was able to breathe easier. He decided to just sit there and wait for Bags to come in, because he was in no shape to get up on Duke's back and go looking for the deputy.

Later on he got into a poker game with a few of the townspeople, played without really paying full attention to the game, but won anyway. He was still playing when Bags walked in.

"That's all for me, boys," Clint said, "but I'd like to keep this table if you fellas don't mind."

They didn't, and moved the game to a nearby empty table. Bags spotted Clint, got himself a beer, and joined him at the table.

"Where've you been?" Clint asked.

"What are you doing up?" Bags countered.

"I got tired of lying down," he replied. "Now suppose you answer my question."

"I went out to see Zack Tyler."

"Damn it, Bags—" Clint stopped when he felt a sharp pain in his side.

"You better just relax and let me tell it," Bags said. "I thought about what you said, about Tyler not making a try on me until he'd made his offer."

"But he made his offer," Clint argued.

"Through Mayor Tidyman," Bags said. "I figured he'd make one more on his own."

"And you were right?"

"He notified me, through one of his hands, that he wanted to see me, so I went out."

"And?"

"We talked," Bags said, and told Clint exactly what had happened. . . .

Bags had ridden out to the Big T spread, been admitted through the front gate without a problem, and left his horse with a hand outside the house. When he went in, he was met by Fran Tyler.

"Hello, Miss Tyler."

"Deputy," she said. "My father is in the room at the head of the stairs, waiting for you. You can go right up."

Bags went up the steps, found the room and knocked on the already open door.

"Come on in," Zack Tyler called.

Bags walked in and faced the man who was sitting up in bed, looking like death warmed over.

"Are you this deputy who is running against my son in the election?" the old man demanded.

"Bags is my name."

"Where do you get off thinking you should be sheriff?" Zack Tyler demanded.

"It's my right to run for the office," Bags said, "but it's up to the people to decide if I should be sheriff."

"Hell—it's my town and I decide who should be sheriff!"

"That's very democratic of you."

"Don't sass me, boy," Tyler said. "I've whipped my boys within an inch of their lives!"

"I'm not one of your boys, Zack," Bags said. "If you've got an offer to make to me, make it and get it over with."

Zack stared at Bags for a long time, and Bags was about to turn around and walk out when the old man finally decided to speak.

"I don't want you making waves in my town, boy," Zack said. "I'll pay you a thousand dollars to forget this election and leave."

"A thousand?" Bags asked. "Is that all it's worth to you?"

"That's more than you'd make in two years as a sheriff," Zack Tyler said.

"Hell, three years," Bags said, "but it still ain't enough to make me back off. I've got my heart set on a career as a lawman."

"So, go on being a deputy," Zack said.

"Not good enough," Bags said. "I think I'll stick around and see how I do."

Bags started out the door when the old man shouted, "All right, damn it. Two thousand!"

Bags waved a hand behind him and kept going.

"Twenty-five hundred!" the old man shouted. "And that's my last offer."

Bags started down the steps.

"You better take it, boy!"

Bags reached the bottom.

"You'll be sorry if you don't!" the old man screeched, but if he spoke after that Bags didn't hear him, because he had gone out the door, mounted up and headed back to town. . . .

"You turned down twenty-five hundred dollars?"

Bags shrugged and said, "Maybe he went higher, but I was gone by then."

"You want to be sheriff that bad?"

"When you think about it, it really isn't that much money," Bags said, and Clint wondered who he was trying to convince. "I'd probably drink, gamble and whore that money away in no time."

"Maybe," Clint said. "But that's an awful lot of drinking, gambling and whoring."

"Well," Bags said, leaning back in his chair, "I figure I could do that here, as sheriff, if I watch my step."

"Has this town got a cathouse?" Clint asked.

"That's right," Bags said. "You don't pay for yours, so you wouldn't now. Sure, Tylerville's got a right nice whorehouse, and they don't charge lawmen."

"That's nice of them."

"Sure is," Bags said. "That could make a man's job a might easier for him."

"That's not the only reason you're determined to stay, though," Clint said.

"Hell, no," Bags said. "You should have seen that old man's face when I walked out on him, Clint. I thought he was gonna have a heart attack right there and then." Bags finished his beer, put the empty mug down. "Why, I'll bet he ups and does have a heart attack when I become the next sheriff."

"If you live that long," Clint said, half under his breath. "Now that you've turned him down—and rudely—he might try and kill you."

"Oh," Bags said, getting up to get another beer, "he already did. Do you want another beer?"

Chapter Twenty-Nine

When Bags returned with the beers he told a stunned Gunsmith the rest of the story.

"Not much to tell, really," he said. "On my way back to town somebody took a shot at me."

"Well, old Zack certainly didn't waste any time," Clint said, "if it was him who set it up."

"Who else could it have been?"

"Jack Tyler, for one," Clint offered.

"I don't think so," Bags said.

"Why not?"

"I've worked with the guy for a while, Clint," Bags said. "He might be coasting in his job, enforcing the law when it suits him, but I don't think he'd stoop to murder to get me out of the election."

"He almost let me be murdered the other night," Clint said. "If it wasn't for you, I would be dead."

"That was different, I think," Bags said. "All he really had to do the other night was not do anything. I don't think he was waiting out there to take a shot at me after my meeting with his old man."

"So then Zack sent someone out there to take a shot at you," Clint said, "only how did the gunman know you hadn't been bought?"

"They might have had some kind of signal worked out," Bags said.

"But if the old man is restricted to his bed, that means there were two others involved, one to give the signal and the other to fire—how many shots?"

"Just one," Bags said. "I didn't hang around to give them a second chance."

"Maybe they missed you deliberately, trying to scare you," Clint suggested. "How close did the shot come?"

"I've got a nice crease in my saddle to show you," Bags said.

"Man'd have to be a hell of a shot to do that on purpose," Clint said.

"I think the guy was doing his damnedest to knock me out of my saddle," Bags said.

"What do you know about Zack Tyler's other two sons?" Clint asked.

"Cliff runs the ranch," Bags said, "and, from what I hear, he also runs the youngest boy, Ben."

"Can either one of them shoot?"

Bags shrugged. "I don't know."

"Why don't you try and find out?" Clint suggested. "Mention the incident to your boss, and bounce it around with him. See what he comes up with."

"He's not going to incriminate his brothers no matter how he feels about them."

"Not deliberately," Clint said, "but maybe he'll say something that will help us."

"Us?" Bags asked. "You're sticking around, then?"

"I told you I was, didn't I?" Clint replied. "You don't think a cracked rib would make me go back on my word?"

"Me?" Bags asked. "I'd never think such a thing."

"Besides," Clint said, "I didn't like the way Jack Tyler handled the situation with Frank Bell. I much preferred your solution. I think you'll make a hell of a sheriff, Bags. Let's see what we can do about getting you the job."

The campaign took on a full head of steam from that

time on, and for that reason, so did Jack Tyler's. In fact, Clint had the distinct impression that Tyler was enjoying the competition. Both men were making speeches every few days, and then, suddenly, Zack Tyler's money showed through.

"A barbecue," Joe Bags told Clint Adams at breakfast. "Zack is having a barbecue at his ranch, in support of his son's campaign."

"Tyler is accepting that from his old man?" Clint asked.

Bags shrugged. "It ain't money, outright. Zack ain't really buying his son the election, he's just playing host to some of his son's supporters."

"Buying votes, that's what he's doing," Clint grumbled, "with food and liquor."

"I can't match that," Bags said.

"Well, there's one thing you can do," Clint said.

"What's that?"

"You can be there."

"I ain't invited," Bags said.

"The whole town's invited, Bags," Clint said. "That's what it's for."

"Old Zack ain't gonna take to the idea," Bags predicted.

"The man isn't a fool, Bags," Clint said. "He'll expect you to come—and me, too."

"You? Why?"

"By now he's figured out that I'm more than passing through," Clint said. "What other reason could I have to stay than to help you stay alive until the election? Maybe he even thinks that you've hired my gun."

"Where would I get the money?" Bags asked.

"I don't know," Clint said, standing up, "but if you get some, let me know. Maybe we can work something out."

"You wouldn't—" Bags started to protest, but he had to rise and pursue the Gunsmith in order to continue.

Chapter Thirty

The barbecue was a gala event, with banners and posters declaring Jack Tyler as the ideal choice for sheriff of Tylerville.

"What a circus," Bags said.

"You ever been to a circus?" Clint asked.

"Once."

"Then you know that there's always a danger that the animals will get out of hand."

Bags turned to look at Clint's face and said, "And what does that mean?"

"I don't know, but here comes the ringmaster," the Gunsmith replied.

Bags looked to where Clint was pointing and saw Fran Tyler pushing a wheelchair with Zack Tyler in it. The old man had a blanket across his legs, and looked shrunken and puny, but the scowl on his face would have scared a ghost. As bad as it was, it deepened when he saw Bags and Clint.

"You know what I notice?" Clint said. "The sheriff isn't here."

Bags looked around him, then said, "You know, you're right."

"I guess Tyler didn't mind his old man throwing a shindig in his honor, but he wasn't about to attend it himself."

"He must really hate the old man," Clint said.

"There's Cliff," Clint said, as he caught sight of the middle son. "He's eyeing us pretty good."

"Speaking of that," Bags said, "little Fran is eyeing you pretty good, too."

Clint looked over at Fran, who turned her eyes away. He hadn't seen or spoken to her since the day of the picnic, and he didn't know if that was her choice or her father's.

"Something going on that I should know about?" Bags asked.

"Nope," Clint said. "Just keep your eyes peeled for the other brother, Ben."

"You don't think they'd try something here, do you?" Bags asked. "Not on their own spread."

"I don't know," Clint said, "but it don't hurt to be on the careful side."

Clint and Bags tried to stay on the outskirts of the crowd. Bags still wasn't sure that they had done the right thing by coming, but Clint kept telling him that it was important for him to put in an appearance.

"Have we put in enough of one?" Bags finally asked.

"Why?"

"I'm hungry, but I'm damned if I'll eat Zack Tyler's food. Let's go back to town and eat at the café, or the hotel."

"Might as well," Clint said.

As they turned to leave, Clint heard someone coming up behind them. He turned in time to see Ben Tyler, the biggest of the three sons.

"Bags."

As Bags turned in response, Ben approached and threw a right that struck the deputy on the butt of the jaw, knocking him to the ground.

"What the hell—" Clint said.

"You insulted my sister," Ben Tyler shouted.

Clint caught on immediately. Ben appeared to be slightly drunk, but Clint knew that he was only supposed to appear so. The Tylers were looking to put Bags in a bad light with the townspeople who were present. First, to make them think that he had insulted a young lady, and second, by giving him a public beating designed to prove that he couldn't even protect himself, let alone a whole town.

"Stand up, Deputy," Ben said. "I'm gonna teach you some manners."

A crowd began to gather, and Clint saw Fran wheel her father over to watch. Cliff Tyler also moved in to observe the proceedings, as well as Mayor Tidyman and several members of the town council, whose opinions would carry great weight with some of the voters.

Clint went over to help Bags to his feet.

"I ought to put a bullet—" the deputy started to say.

"That would suit their purpose even more," Clint said. "Zack would probably love it, even though it would cost him a son."

"Then what am I supposed to do?" Bags asked, wiping his bloody lip with the back of his hand.

"You'll have to fight him," Clint said.

"Fight him?" Bags repeated. "In case you haven't noticed, he's a might bigger than a breadbox."

"So was Frank Bell," Clint said, "and you saw what I did to him."

"He almost killed you!" Bags hissed.

"Yeah, but I hurt him some first," Clint said.

Bags looked Ben Tyler up and down, and then said, "I still think I ought to plug him."

"Sure. Maybe you could get around behind him and shoot him in the ass," Clint said. "Give me your gun, Bags. You can see he ain't wearing one."

Bags looked and saw that, sure enough, Ben Tyler had shucked his gunbelt, which was in his brother Cliff's left hand.

"Damn it," Bags said. "How is taking a beating gonna help my chances?"

"It won't," Clint said, taking Bags's gunbelt and slinging it over his shoulder, "but backing down would hurt them more. Just go ahead and take your best shot, Bags."

"Shit," was the deputy's reply.

"You gonna fight or walk, Deputy?"

"I didn't insult your sister, Ben Tyler," Bags said, "but if you insist on a fight, I'll give you one."

"If I whup you, then you sure enough insulted my sister," Ben said.

"And I guess it works the other way around," Clint spoke up. "If he whips you, he didn't."

"Fair enough!" Cliff Tyler called out, grinning. "I ain't met the man yet could whup Ben in a fair fight."

"Fair fight," Bags muttered. "He's already cheating sixty pounds worth."

"Who told you to grow up so skinny?" Clint said. "Just stay away from the reach of his arms, Bags. Remember my rib."

"Yeah," Bags said. "Remember my face, because it sure as hell ain't gonna look the same after this."

The deputy raised his fists and stepped forward, with a sinking feeling in his stomach.

He wondered fleetingly if old man Zack Tyler had that twenty-five hundred dollars on him.

Chapter Thirty-One

Bags moved in on big Ben Tyler, who stood his ground, arms hanging loose at his side.

"Gonna give you a free shot, Deputy," Ben said, "because I owe you one, but after that I'm gonna take your head off."

"You're gonna try," Bags said.

"Go ahead," Ben said, sticking out his lantern jaw. "Take your free punch."

I hope I don't break my hand, Bags thought.

There were better targets available, but Bags found that he couldn't resist that jutting jaw, so he hauled off and threw a punch with all of his one hundred and sixty pounds behind it. As his fist exploded on Ben Tyler's jaw, it felt as if he'd punched a stone wall. Ben took a half a step backward, but he didn't blink and he sure as hell didn't fall.

"That's it, Deputy," Ben said. He brought his hands up so that they were no longer dangling at his side and said, "It's time to teach you some better manners."

"Shit," Bags muttered. His hand was throbbing painfully, but he dared not let on, and he also dared not baby it. He was going to need both hands if he was gonna come out of this in one piece—one bruised and battered piece, that is.

Bags tried to use his speed by stepping in and peppering

Ben with punches, the way Clint had done with Frank Bell, but the big man was virtually unaffected. At one point, as Bags stepped in, Ben swung a wicked backhanded left that caught Bags on the shoulder and knocked him down. Ben stepped in then and tried to stomp Bags into the ground, but the deputy rolled away.

"You said a fair fight, Tyler," Clint shouted at Cliff. "I think your brother just changed the rules."

Cliff Tyler just lifted his hands in a helpless gesture.

"I ain't got no control over my younger brother, Adams," Cliff said.

"The rules have changed," Clint said. "Do you hear me, Bags?"

"I hear you," Bags said under his breath.

His shoulder was throbbing now where Ben had caught him, and he stood up to meet the big man's advance.

"Gonna take your head off," Ben said.

"You're gonna have to do it from your knees," Bags muttered. He threw a kick, raising the front of his foot so that it was the heel of his boot that caught Ben Tyler flush on the right kneecap. The man's mouth opened and as he bent over to clutch at his knee, Bags kicked out with his toe, this time, catching Ben on the side of the jaw. The big man staggered back, and his knee gave way, causing him to fall.

"Come on, big man," Bags shouted, and Clint shook his head. False bravado had gotten the best of Bags. He should have moved in on Ben while the big man was down, but instead he gave him a chance to stagger back to his feet. Clint hoped that the decision wouldn't come back to haunt the deputy.

Ben Tyler got back to his feet and wiped a smear of blood off his face with his sleeve. His jaw was swelling up and turning black where Bags's toe had caught him, and he still couldn't put all of his weight on his injured knee, but that didn't stop him from coming forward.

Bags stepped in again, threw some punches at Ben's

face again, but the bigger man warded them off with his elbows, and then swung a mean right that landed on Bags's left eye.

Bags backed off blindly. The punch couldn't have landed in a worse spot. Momentarily blind, Bags tried to back away from the big man's charge, but was bowled over by a lowered shoulder. On the ground he caught a kick in the side that lifted him off the ground, but in throwing the kick he put too much weight on his throbbing knee, and fell to the ground himself.

"Idiot!" Cliff breathed.

Both men were on the ground now, Ben clutching his knee again and Bags squinting out of one eye.

"Kick, damn it," Clint said, loud enough for only himself to hear.

Things were obviously not going the way the Tyler clan had planned so he kept a wary eye on both Cliff and Zack.

Bags scrambled around onto his back and, locating Ben with his one good eye, lashed out with a vicious kick that caught the man just under his chin, in the throat.

Ben made a horrible choking noise, and Clint saw Cliff's hand streak towards his gun.

"Don't," he called out, and Cliff looked over at the Gunsmith and stayed his hand.

Ben was lying on his back with his hands to his throat, fighting to get some breath into him.

"It's over," Clint said, "unless you want Bags to stomp your brother while he's helpless."

Cliff didn't answer, and Clint suspected that the man wouldn't have minded that so much at all.

"It's finished," Zack spoke up, and Clint looked at the old man in surprise. "The deputy didn't insult my daughter."

He said something else that only Fran heard and, with a fleeting glance toward the Gunsmith, she turned her father's chair around and wheeled him back toward the house.

Clint went over to Bags, who still couldn't see through his left eye.

"What happened?" Bags asked.

"It's all over."

"Who won?"

"You did. How do you feel?"

"Sore."

"You still hungry?"

Bags thought about it a moment, then said, "Damned if I ain't."

"Well, here's your gun. Let's go on back to town and get something to eat." Clint took a close look at Bags's face then and added, "I guess we ought to stop by the doc's first, though. You'll want to see what you're eating."

Chapter Thirty-Two

Clint stared across the table at Joe Bags, whose left eye was swollen completely shut. Bags looked up at Clint with his one good eye and said, "Stop staring at me."

"I can't help it," Clint said. "I'm terribly impressed."

"Shit!"

"My only question is, when you had him down the first time, why didn't you move in?"

Looking sheepish, Bags admitted, "I got carried away."

"You almost did," Clint told him. "Next time you've got a man hurt, move in on him and finish him, or he might finish you."

"I'll remember."

"How do you feel?"

Bags shrugged. "My hand's puffed up some." He raised his swollen right hand. "My shoulder hurts, and I can't see too good, but all in all I'd say I felt pretty good."

"You should," Clint said. "I'm pretty sure you won yourself some votes today."

"I hope so."

At that point Clint saw Sheriff Jack Tyler enter the café. He looked around, located them and then started over.

When he reached the table he took a close look at Bags's face and said, "I guess it's true."

"What is?" Bags asked.

"You tangled with my brother Ben and came out of it in one piece," Tyler said.

"He did more than that," Clint said.

"Yeah, I heard that, too, but I didn't believe it," the sheriff said. Looking back at Bags he said, "What I want to know is, why didn't you arrest him?"

"What?"

"He hit you first, didn't he?" Tyler said, louder than Clint thought necessary.

"Well, yeah, but—"

"You're a peace officer, damn it," Jack said, louder now. "He hit you and you should have locked him up."

"He's your brother," Bags said, and Clint covered his eyes with his hand. He had a lot of respect for Jack Tyler, all of a sudden. The man was smarter than he had realized.

"I don't care whose brother he is, Bags," the sheriff continued. "Next time someone breaks the law, you lock him up. That is, if you want to keep wearing that badge. You understand?"

Frowning, Bags said, "Sure, Sheriff, I understand."

"Good," Tyler said. "Go on with your meal, then, and then make your rounds, if you feel fit enough."

"I'm fit enough," Bags said.

The sheriff nodded once, then turned and left the café.

"What the hell was that all about?" Bags asked.

"Look around you," Clint said, leaning his chin on the base of his right palm.

Bags looked around and saw that he was the center of attraction. All of the other diners were looking at him.

"That man," Clint said, "just lost you some votes. I think you broke just about even today, Bags—if you're lucky."

Chapter Thirty-Three

When Clint got back to his hotel that night he sensed a presence in the darkened hall and his hand moved towards his gun.

"Clint," a woman's voice called. He recognized it and relaxed his gun hand.

"Fran?"

"Yes."

He approached his door and she came to him and pressed herself against him with her head on his chest.

"I'm sorry," she said.

"For what?" he asked, genuinely perplexed by the apology.

"That I haven't been to see you," she explained, "even after you were hurt. My father told my brothers—my half brothers—that he didn't want me coming to town to see you. I haven't been successful in sneaking away until tonight. I'm glad I came." She pressed even closer to his chest.

"Let's get out of the hall," Clint suggested. He eased her away so that he could get to his key, then opened the door and allowed her to slip in ahead of him.

Once inside Clint turned up the lamp and looked at Fran Tyler.

"How's the deputy?" she asked.

"He's all right," Clint said. "Be a while before he can see out of his left eye, but other than that he's fine. What about Ben?"

"Ben's never been whipped before," she said. "He got drunk tonight and Cliff is watching out for him. That's the only reason I was able to get away tonight."

"Why is he watching out for him?" Clint asked.

"Ben wanted to take his gun, come into town and shoot the deputy," she explained. "My father doesn't want that."

"He doesn't want the deputy shot?"

She thought about that a moment, then answered. "That's not what I said. He doesn't want Ben coming in and shooting the deputy in front of the whole town."

"What about from ambush?"

Fran shrugged. "I don't try and predict what any of them will do."

"Well, somebody took a shot at Bags the other day after he left your father."

"I don't know anything about that," Fran said. "All I know is that I've been thinking about you ever since our picnic."

"I've thought about you, too," Clint said.

"Good."

She was wearing riding clothes, and now she started to slowly slip out of them. Clint watched as the shadows played over her body, the deepest ones nestling between her breasts and thighs.

"Now you," she said, breathlessly.

"I don't know if I'm in shape for this, Fran," he said. He unbuttoned his shirt and opened it to show her the bandages.

She moved close to him so she could run her hands over the bandages. "Let me help you, then," she said, and began to undress him.

When she had all of his clothes removed she guided him

to the bed. "You just lie back and let me do it. I'll try not to hurt you."

She helped him lower himself to the bed gently, then began to run her hands over his body, pausing at his genitals, cupping, stroking, squeezing, making it virtually impossible for Clint to lie perfectly still.

"Be still," she said, but when she lowered her mouth onto him, he lifted his hips to meet her. She continued to stroke him while she ministered to him with her mouth.

She moved her mouth off of his cock and began to run her lips over his bandaged torso, cupping his testicles in her hand.

"I want to climb on top of you," she whispered. "I want you inside me. I'll try not to hurt you."

She got on the bed with him, straddled him and then sat across his hips, flattening his erection between them. She was testing her weight to see if it would hurt him.

"Is it all right?"

"It's fine," he said. He could feel the heat of her on his stiff organ, and he reached for her, wanting to lift her so he could slip inside her.

"I'll do it," she said, pushing his hands away gently. "I'll do it all."

Putting her weight on her knees, she raised herself up and allowed the swollen tip of his cock to prod her moist opening.

"Who are you teasing?" he asked.

"I just want it to last."

She teased both of them a little more, then allowed him to sink into the steaming hot depths of her, an inch at a time.

"Ahhh," she said, squeezing her eyes shut, drawing the sound out, like a man taking a drink after just coming off a desert.

"Is it all right?" she asked again.

"Yes."

She wiggled her hips and asked, ''Is it good?''

''Oh, yes,'' he said, and she laughed, drew herself up until he was almost out of her, then eased back down again.

He reached up then and cupped her firm breasts in his hands, enjoying the feel of the hardened nipples against his palms.

''Squeeze them,'' she said, ''hard.''

He did as she asked, squeezing her breasts in his hands, and at the same time flicked at her nipples with his thumbs. She closed her eyes and began to churn her hips, wiggling him around inside of her.

The movement of her hips was starting to get a little frenzied, causing Clint some discomfort in the rib area, but that was the only place he felt anything but great pleasure. She was clenching and unclenching her muscles, sucking him deeper and deeper inside of her while he continued to caress her breasts, and suddenly her entire body tensed, and then shuddered, and when he began to fill her up, she caught her breath and leaned into his hands, and they ended with her lying flat on top of him.

She licked the sweat from his neck and asked, ''How do you feel?''

''Fine,'' he said. Then, running his hands over her back, her rump and the back of her thighs he said, ''You feel fine, too.''

''I feel wonderful,'' she said, ''but I think I'd better get off of you carefully, just to be on the safe side.''

Working together they managed to get her off of him without causing him too much pain, and when she was lying next to him she nestled her head against his shoulder and went to sleep.

Clint did not go to sleep right away. He did some thinking about the Tylers—all of them—and decided that the most dangerous one of all, and the one to watch, was Cliff. Apparently, he had some control over Ben, who was physically the most imposing, and he had not appeared to be too intimidated by his father at the barbecue. In fact, Clint suspected that the whole idea of accusing Bags of insulting Fran had been Cliff Tyler's.

Oddly enough, the least dangerous of the Tylers seemed to be Sheriff Jack, who probably had the most to lose, personally. All Zack would lose was having a son as sheriff. He would still own the town.

Fran made a small sound, just enough to remind Clint of her presence, and thinking about some of the women in his past, he had to conclude that the female Tyler could conceivably turn out to be the most dangerous of all. She hadn't seemed too willing to talk about her half brothers' possible involvement in the attempt on Joe Bags's life. In fact, she had gotten off the subject pretty quick, using a woman's most effective weapon—her body.

Just before he finally drifted off to sleep, Clint decided that maybe he and Fran should have a talk in a somewhat more neutral situation.

Chapter Thirty-Four

Zack Tyler had to call out three times before Cliff finally came into the room.

"Where the hell have you been?" Zack demanded. "I been yelling like a coyote."

"I know," Cliff said. "I've been downstairs, trying to sit on Ben."

"Does that idiot still want to go to town and shoot the deputy?" Zack demanded.

"He did," Cliff said, "but I finally got enough liquor into him to put him to sleep."

"Well, then, get me something to eat."

"Where's Fran?"

"She went into town," Zack said.

"I thought you didn't want her—"

"Don't question my decisions, boy," Zack interrupted. "Just go downstairs and get me something to eat."

Cliff stood his ground and put his hands on his hips, staring at the old man.

"Are you gonna defy me, boy?"

"I was considering it," Cliff said, honestly, "but it wouldn't do any good."

"Damn right it wouldn't," Zack said.

In his mind's eye Cliff could see himself drawing his gun and firing one shot at the old man, drilling him through the head, splattering the wall behind him with Zack Tyler's blood and brains, and making a whole lot of people happy. It seemed such an easy thing to do, yet he knew he wouldn't do it—and love for his father had nothing to do with it. Cliff still had some things to learn before he could run the ranch and the town as well—or better—than the old man had been doing.

"Well?" Zack said, breaking into Cliff's reverie.

"I'll get you something to eat," Cliff said. He started out, then turned back and said, "Oh, when will Fran be back?"

"I don't know," Zack said. "If she does what I want, she might not be back all night."

Cliff frowned at the old buzzard, wondering what was running around in his head now, then left to get old Zack his dinner.

When Clint woke up and found Fran Tyler sitting in a chair, fully dressed, watching him, he became annoyed at himself. Even allowing for the cracked rib, he should not have been sleeping soundly enough for her to have gotten out of bed and moved about the room without waking him.

I must be getting old, he thought, as he struggled to sit up.

"Good morning," she said.

He had his own opinion about that, but he said, "Good morning," in reply.

"Do you want some help?"

"I'm fine," he said. "Why don't you go downstairs and wait for me in the dining room, and we'll have some breakfast—that is, if you don't mind anybody seeing you—"

"I don't mind," Fran said, standing up. "I'll wait for you downstairs. We have to talk," she added, seriously.

"I agree."

Clint didn't know what she had in mind. He only hoped she wasn't going to say she loved him, or something along those lines. He didn't need that sort of involvement in his life. It had happened a few times before, and nothing good had ever come of it.

When she went out the door he struggled to his feet, washed up in the basin and got dressed, wishing he could take off the bandages so he could take a bath. He'd have to take that up with Dr. Madonna later on.

Strapping on his gun he left the room and went down to the dining room, expecting to find Fran Tyler.

He was disappointed.

He called over one of the waitresses and asked if she had seen Fran Tyler. The answer was no.

Where had she gone? And why?

He went through the lobby and outside where he looked up and down the street. She couldn't have gotten that far.

He was about to step off the boardwalk when he stopped himself. What the hell was he chasing after her for? She was the one who had come to him, and then run out on him. He had the feeling that she had come to him for more than just a night in bed, and that afterwards she had second thoughts.

The only question now was, had she come to help him, or hurt him? Had she come on her own, or had Zack sent her? Either way, she was gone now, and if she really had something on her mind, she'd be back to share it with him.

He went back into the hotel to have breakfast, after which he sought out the doctor to ask him about the tape on his ribs.

"What's the difference?" Madonna asked. "You won't listen to me anyway."

"Look, Doc, just tell me if I can take the tape off or not," Clint said.

"Sure, you can take it off," the doctor said. "What do you want to do, wrestle with someone?"

"Only if it's a female," Clint said. "Actually, what I want to do is take a hot bath."

"Now that you mention it," Madonna said, "that

might not be a bad idea. I'll unwrap you, and you go get into a hot bath.'' The doctor kept talking while he was unwrapping. ''After that, see how you feel. If you've got pain, come back and we'll wrap you up tight, again.''

''Oh, no,'' Clint said. ''Once I'm out of this thing, I'm out.''

''Well,'' the doctor said, slipping off the last loop of bandages, ''you're out.''

Clint stood up and stretched experimentally. Initially there was a stab of pain, but it faded away to a dull ache, and he actually felt pretty good—and said so.

''Well, you should,'' Madonna said, probing Clint's side with his fingers. ''I'm a hell of a doctor.''

Clint rubbed his hand over his side—it *itched*—and said, ''I won't argue with you there, Doc.''

''No,'' Madonna said, ''but you'll argue when you get my bill.''

Clint slipped his shirt back on, but did not button it, as he was heading straight for a bath.

''Thanks for getting me unwrapped, Doc,'' Clint said. ''You send me your bill and I'll be glad to pay it.''

''That I've got to see,'' Madonna said, ''somebody glad to pay me. Take care of yourself, Mr. Adams. I don't want anybody saying I treated a legend, and then he died.''

Clint frowned, both at the ''legend'' remark and the part about dying.

''Who says I'm going to die, Doc?'' Clint asked.

''Nobody,'' Madonna said. ''And if you want to know who says you're a legend, everybody.'' The doctor saw that Clint was serious and said, ''Hey, I was just making a joke.''

''Yeah,'' Clint said. ''Some joke. Men like me don't joke about death, Doc,'' he added. ''I would have thought the same was true for doctors.''

Clint headed for the door, stopped with his hand on the doorknob and said, ''Thanks, again.''

Chapter Thirty-Five

Clint was soaking in the tub when the sheriff walked in. It was a split second before Clint identified his visitor as Tyler, but that was enough time for him to draw his gun from his holster which was hanging on the back of a chair next to the tub.

"I guess you're as fast as they say," Tyler said, showing his palms to indicate that his hands were empty.

Clint didn't answer; he just holstered his gun and returned to his soak.

"Mind if I sit down for a few minutes?"

"You're the sheriff," Clint said.

"Yeah," Tyler said, "but maybe not for long, huh?"

Clint opened his eyes and looked at Tyler. "What's that mean?"

"Well, there are a lot of people in this town who don't like my old man," Tyler said. He reversed a chair and sat with his arms draped on the back. "A lot of them see this election as a chance to get out from under him, you know? For the first time, they're thinking they've got a way to beat him."

"So? What's your point?"

"I don't rightly know," Tyler said. "Maybe I'm just talking out loud to hear myself, you know?"

"What do you think about that attempt on Bags's life?" Clint asked.

"What about it?"

"You think your brothers could have tried it, on instructions from your father?"

"It's possible," Tyler said, after a moment's thought. "If the old man thought I might lose the election, he might look at it the same way as some of the townspeople."

"The beginning of the end, you mean?"

"Yeah."

"What are your feelings about this, Tyler?" Clint asked.

"The election, you mean?"

"Yes."

"I never wanted this job, Adams," Jack Tyler said. "I'd much rather be running the ranch."

"Why aren't you?"

"I think my brother Cliff convinced the old man that he should have one of his sons wearing a badge in this town," Jack said. "Cliff's a smart boy. Give the badge to your oldest son, he'd say, I don't mind, and then he ends up with the ranch."

"What about Ben?"

"Ben does whatever Cliff says."

"And Cliff does whatever Zack says?"

"Not always," Tyler said. "Cliff is intimidated the least of all of us by the old man."

"Why is that?"

Jack shrugged. "I guess it's because he thinks more like old Zack than any of the rest of us do."

Clint rubbed his hand over his side and asked, "Why are you telling me this, Sheriff?"

"Sheriff," Jack repeated, half to himself. "I don't really know, Adams. I guess I just want you to know that I intend to try and win this election on my own. If anything funny happens—"

"—you had nothing to do with it, right?"

"Right," Jack said, standing up. "That's all I wanted to say."

"Okay," Clint replied. "You said it."

"Yeah." Tyler looked like he wanted to say more, but instead he just waved a hand halfheartedly and left.

Clint leaned his head back against the rim of the tub and wondered about Jack Tyler. Maybe he didn't think like his old man, but he was smart. He could have been trying to put Clint and Bags off their guard.

Was he telling the truth about not really wanting the job as sheriff? You couldn't have guessed that from the way he had torn into Bags in the café the day before. Why such a change of heart from one day to the next?

Why a change of heart at all?

Would the real Jack Tyler please stand up?

Chapter Thirty-Six

"These Tylers are driving me a little nuts," Clint told Joe Bags later.

"So there *is* something going on between you and little Fran," Bags said.

"There's something going on with Fran, with Jack, with Cliff," Clint said. "Zack's the only one I can read all right—and Ben. Zack wants to keep the town—and his sons—underneath his thumb, and Ben just does what Cliff tells him."

"So what about the other three?"

"They're not so easy," Clint said.

It was afternoon, and they were sitting in the saloon, each nursing a beer. Bags's eye was still swollen and purplish, but he was able to see through it slightly.

"Fran's hard to figure," Clint went on, "but then she's a woman. They're always hard to figure."

"That's the truth," Bags agreed.

"Jack and Cliff, they're a different story. According to Jack, Cliff thinks the same way old Zack does, so he's probably out to take Zack's place when the old man dies."

"And what does Jack want?"

"In spite of what he says, maybe all he wants is to be sheriff of Tylerville."

"Bad enough to kill for it?"

"Well, the closer we get to the election, the better

chance we have of finding that out, don't we?'' Clint asked. ''If I were you I'd figure on staying around town until it's all over. If somebody wants to make another try for you, they're going to have to have the nerve to do it right in town, where we can catch him.''

''Sure,'' Bags said, ''after he kills me.''

''After he *tries*.'' Clint frowned at his friend and asked, ''Are you having second thoughts about this, now?''

''Maybe a few,'' Bags admitted. ''But not enough to back down from it. I'll see it through.''

''Don't stick around on my account,'' Clint said, quickly. ''If you want out just say the word and we can forget it. You can go back to being deputy, or you can leave town the same time I do.''

Bags stared into his mug at the remains of his beer.

''Think about it, Bags,'' Clint said. ''Don't let pride make you stay.''

''It's not pride,'' Bags argued, ''not really. ''It's just something that I want to do, something that I started and now I have to finish it. Does that make sense?''

''Sure,'' Clint told him. ''Everybody likes to finish what they start . . . as long as what you start doesn't end up finishing you,'' he added.

Bags looked at Clint. ''I think I'll stick it out, Clint— which doesn't mean that you have to stay around if you don't want to.''

''Well, I'm kind of the same way you are, Bags,'' Clint said. ''I like to finish what I start, too.'' He raised his mug, with what little was left of his beer in it. ''We'll stick it out together.''

Chapter Thirty-Seven

From that point on Clint Adams virtually became Deputy Joe Bags's shadow. It might have been wiser, from one point of view, if Bags had given up his job as deputy so that he wouldn't have to make regular rounds—making himself an easier target—but on the other hand, quitting like that could cost him votes, so they decided against that course of action.

Clint also decided that, until the election, it would be better if they both bunked together, but not at the hotel. After some thought, he proposed that they move into his rig in the livery stable and sleep there.

"Somebody could just slip into the stable and fill that rig full of lead, Clint," Bags suggested.

"Not while Duke is there," Clint said. "Nobody is going to slip past him without him raising a ruckus. I think it's a good idea, Bags, but if you don't like it—"

"No, no, whatever you say," Bags said. "I'm leaving it to you to keep me alive at least long enough to pin that sheriff's badge on."

As the days went by, it seemed that Joe Bags's popularity, and his chances, were growing. There were at least as many signs up in plain sight supporting him as there were supporting Jack Tyler. It seemed that the fight with Ben Tyler out at the Big T had worked against the interests of

147

the Tylers and increased Bags's popularity once the word got around.

About three days before the election, Bags was scheduled to make a speech.

"I wish we could skip this one," Clint said, "but it's too close to the election to do that."

"Why skip it?"

"It'll be dark soon," Clint said. "This is the last speech you'll make after dark before the election. The street will be lit by torches, but it's still a good time for somebody to try and kill you."

"Well, fine," Bags said. "That helps me concentrate on what I've got to say."

"You concentrate on what you've got to say," Clint said, "and I'll concentrate on keeping you alive. That's our deal, right?"

"Sure, but you don't mind if I worry a little, do you?" Bags asked.

"Why not?" Clint asked, and then added, "Especially since I'm worried a lot."

A platform—which almost resembled a gallows platform—had been erected for both candidates to make speeches from. That night Jack Tyler was scheduled to make a speech right after Bags. The platform was surrounded by burning torches, and the moment Bags stepped inside the circle, he'd be a perfect target for a rifleman on any rooftop across the way.

Jack Tyler came early and stood among the crowd to hear what Joe Bags had to say.

While Bags spoke, Clint hardly heard him. His eyes were scanning rooftops and windows, looking for any sign of a man with a gun taking a bead on the deputy. When Bags was finished, the crowd applauded, signaling the Gunsmith that his friend was done.

Bags approached him, wiping the perspiration from his brow.

"Hot up there, huh?" Clint asked.

"Hell, yes, it's hot with all those torches," Bags said, "but that ain't why I'm sweating. Can we get out of here now? I need a drink."

"Tyler came for your speech," Clint pointed out, "so you better stay for his."

Bags nodded, and they both faced the platform as the sheriff prepared to speak.

The crowd seemed to Clint to be about split in half between the two candidates, and he had to admit that he was surprised at the amount of support that Bags had been able to accumulate. Apparently the town was genuinely tired of being under Zack Tyler's rule.

Tyler's charm came out during his speech, and Clint found that the man was also an excellent speaker. When the Gunsmith abandoned his thoughts and zeroed in on what the man was saying, he was somewhat surprised.

"I know you people think that a vote for me is a vote for my father, Zack Tyler," he said, and there were some jeers from the crowd. "That's not true. I accepted no help from my father the first time I ran for sheriff, and I've accepted no help from him now."

"What about the barbecue?" somebody from the crowd shouted, and Jack Tyler seemed pleased. Clint wouldn't have been surprised if Tyler himself had planted the question.

"You'll notice I did not attend that barbecue," he told the people. "Somebody wants to have a shindig, that's up to them. All I want you good people to know is that when I wear this badge, *I'm* the sheriff, not Zack Tyler. I've been sheriff for one term now, and for the most part, Tylerville has been a quiet and peaceful town. None of you can deny that."

There was a murmur of assent through the crowd. Clint had to admire the way Jack Tyler was playing to his audience, like an actor.

Was he acting?

"But there's one thing I feel I have to promise you,"

Jack Tyler said, ''and that is that Zack Tyler will have no influence on the office of sheriff as long as I hold it.''

Tyler's supporters started to cheer, and the noise drowned out the shot. The Gunsmith, however, saw the bullet enter Jack Tyler's left arm. He saw the blood start to blossom just before Tyler clapped his hand over it and fell to the ground.

''What the hell?'' Bags shouted.

Clint turned and started scanning the rooftops and windows again, looking for whoever had fired the shot. The tallest building across the street was a feed and grain warehouse that was owned by Zack Tyler.

''Come on,'' Clint told Bags.

''Where?''

''To play a hunch,'' Clint said. ''Follow me.''

Both men drew their guns and rushed across the street while the majority of the crowd rushed forward to the platform.

''The warehouse?'' Bags asked.

''It's the biggest building,'' Clint said, ''and would afford a rifleman his best target. We'll each circle around it in the opposite direction and see what we come up with.''

''All right,'' Bags said. ''Meet you on the other side.''

They split up and began to circle the warehouse. Clint stopped at every door he came to but found them all locked. As he reached the back of the building he flattened himself against the wall, holding his gun up next to his head, and then dashed around the corner to the back.

Nothing.

At that point Joe Bags executed the same maneuver from the other end, and Clint waved him on.

Against the back of the building, secured to the wall, was a ladder leading to the roof.

''I'm going up,'' Clint told Bags. ''You cover me from down here.''

"What if he's still up there?"

"I doubt it," Clint said. "There must be at least one other way down from there. He's got to be long gone by now, unless he's just plain stupid. But let me check the roof anyway."

Bags kept his eyes on the brush out behind the warehouse, just in case the rifleman was in there and chose to fire at Clint while he was climbing the ladder.

Clint had holstered his gun so that he could use both hands for climbing, but when he came within a few rungs of the top he drew it out again, and then climbed the remainder of the way.

He stuck his head and arm up first, scanned as much of the darkened roof as he could that way, then climbed up the rest of the way until he was standing on the roof.

He began to make a slow circuit of the roof, scraping his feet on the ground, looking for spent shells. When he reached the front he looked down at the platform and saw a crowd of people around Sheriff Tyler. From where he was, though, he couldn't tell how Tyler was.

Even though he had not found any evidence, he was convinced that this had to be where the shots had come from. He went back to where the ladder was and called down to Bags.

"I'm going to look for another way inside."

"All right," came the reply from the darkness below.

He started a second circuit of the roof, and finally found what he was looking for—a trap door. He opened it and found a ladder leading down into the bowels of the warehouse. The rifleman could very easily have still been down there, crouched in the darkness, waiting for all of the commotion to blow over so he could leave. It would be foolish to even consider going down there without some kind of light.

Holstering his gun, the Gunsmith lowered himself down until both of his feet were firmly planted on a rung of the ladder. He descended a couple of steps, then reached for the trap door and replaced it above him, leaving himself in total darkness.

He stood at the top of the ladder for a few minutes, just listening for the slightest sound that might tell him if anyone else was in the building with him. Finally, he gave that up and started his descent.

Several times he thought he should have reached the floor already, and found that he still had a way to go. He wished he had counted the rungs on the outside ladder while going up.

Finally, his foot touched down, and he crouched and drew his gun. All he could do now was grope his way around until he found a door leading to the outside.

If he didn't bump into a would-be killer, first.

Chapter Thirty-Eight

"Your rib hurt?" Doc Madonna asked Clint. He'd noticed the Gunsmith absently rubbing his side while they were talking.

"A bit," Clint admitted.

"It's no wonder," Madonna said. "Running, climbing ladders—"

"We're supposed to be talking about Sheriff Tyler's condition, not mine," Clint reminded the man.

"Oh, he's fine," Madonna said. "Took a bullet in the arm, but it passed right through without doing a hell of a lot of damage."

"That means we don't even have a bullet," Bags said.

"We'll have to look for it," Clint replied. "Can we talk to him now?" he asked, addressing himself to the doctor.

"He'll be coming out in a few minutes," the doctor said. "Why don't you take him over to the saloon and buy him a drink? I think he can use it."

"I think we all could," Clint agreed.

A few moments later Jack Tyler came out, awkwardly trying to button his shirt with his right hand while his left hung limply at his side. No one offered to help him.

"How do you feel?" the doctor asked.

"Better than I did," Tyler said. "Thanks, Doc."

"How about a drink, Tyler?" Clint asked. The sheriff

153

looked up at Clint, who added, "I think we've got some talking to do."

"The three of us," Bags added.

Tyler studied both of their faces, then said, "Just let me finish with this damned shirt and we'll be on our way."

When they were all seated at the saloon with a drink in hand Clint said, "We're a little confused here, Sheriff."

"About what?"

"We were under the impression that Bags here was the target, not you," Clint said. "How do you feel about this turn of events?"

Tyler studied them both again, as he had in the doctor's office, then sighed and said, "Confused."

"You've got no idea who could have shot you?"

"None."

"What about your family?"

"I don't think so," he said. "Now, don't get me wrong. I wouldn't put it past any of them, if it would serve a purpose."

"You don't see this," Clint said, indicating the lawman's wound, "as serving any purpose?"

"Not for my family, no," he said, "unless old Zack is getting senile in his old age."

"Or very clever," Bags said.

"He's always been clever," Tyler said. "Or maybe crafty would be a better word."

"And Cliff?"

"Like I said, Cliff is like Zack," Tyler reminded me.

"Would Cliff pull something like this without the old man's okay?" Clint asked.

Jack thought that over for a few moments, and then said, "I wouldn't put it past him—but again, it would have to serve some purpose."

"Maybe he just wants to get you out of the way," Bags suggested.

"I'm not in his way," Jack said. "Cliff is the foreman of the ranch, I'm the sheriff. We're miles apart. We haven't even spoken to each other in weeks.''

"I don't know," Clint said, shaking his head and pouring another drink all around. "I was all geared up for an attempt on Bags. This just doesn't sit right with me."

"Did you find out where the shot came from?" Tyler asked.

"I have to assume that the rifleman was on top of the grain warehouse," Clint said.

"Did you find anything on the roof?"

"No, and I went down into the warehouse, too, and stumbled around in the dark for a while."

"Scared the crap out of me popping out the back door that way," Bags said.

Clint had staggered around inside the warehouse for a few minutes, and when he finally encountered a door and shoved it open, it actually struck Joe Bags in the back.

"Once the door was open," Clint went on, "there was some light inside, but there was still no sign of anyone. He must have gotten off the roof and away before we got there—and we got there pretty damned quick."

"Did you see anything before you were shot?" Bags asked.

Tyler thought back, then shook his head and said, "I didn't see a thing. I was looking at the crowd most of the time."

Playing to the crowd, Clint remembered. "What do you intend to do about this?"

"I'm not a detective," Jack Tyler said, "and I never claimed to be, but I guess I'll have to ask some questions, see if anyone saw anything."

"We can take a look at the platform and see if the bullet lodged anywhere where we can get at it," Clint said. "At least then we'd know what kind of a gun was used."

"What happens if there's some evidence pointing to a member of your family, Jack?" Bags asked. "I know how you all feel about each other, but I also know how you feel about being Tylers."

"I honestly don't know," the sheriff said. "I guess I'll

just have to go out there and question my family. If one of them is trying to kill me, the others won't take kindly to it any more than I do.''

''You're the oldest brother,'' Clint said. ''That alone could be motive enough for Cliff to try and kill you . . . depending on what your father's will says.''

''I don't know what it says,'' Jack Tyler said. ''I think the old man and his lawyer are the only ones who do.''

''Who's his lawyer?''

''Robert Rice,'' Jack said. ''He's got an office right here in town.''

''Too bad we can't find out what that will says,'' Bags lamented.

''Maybe we can,'' Tyler said, suddenly.

''How?'' Bags asked.

''Well, I'm the law here in town, and this is an investigation of an attempted murder.'' Jack stood up and said, ''Bags, meet me in the morning at Rice's office, and we'll see what we can do about getting a look at that will.'' He made a move to leave, then stopped and said, ''You can come, too, Adams. You're pretty involved in all of this.''

''I'm obliged for the invitation, Sheriff,'' Clint said. ''I'll be there.''

Clint watched Jack Tyler walk from the saloon, then poured himself another drink.

''Bags,'' he said to his friend, ''you may be in a little trouble, here.''

''Why do you say that?''

''The longer I know Jack Tyler, and watch him, the more convinced I become that if I was a citizen of this town, I'm not sure who *I* would vote for!''

Bags stared at the Gunsmith and said, ''Well, that's a hell of a thing to say to a friend.''

Clint pushed the bottle of whiskey towards the deputy and said, ''Have a drink, friend.''

Chapter Thirty-Nine

The next morning Clint and Bags met at the Gunsmith's hotel and walked together to the lawyer's office. When they got there they found Sheriff Tyler waiting for them, which impressed Clint even more. When pressed, he thought, Tyler was probably a pretty good sheriff, and now he was being pressed.

"How do you feel?" Clint asked.

"Sore," Tyler said.

"I know what it's like."

"I don't," Tyler said. "This is the first time I've ever been shot, and I don't like it."

"I don't blame you," Clint said. "Shall we go in?"

"Sure, but I'd appreciate it if you fellas would remember that I'm still sheriff and let me do the talking."

"You're the boss," Bags said, and they went in.

Robert Rice turned out to be a man just about the same age as Zack Tyler. He had the same white hair and pale skin, but physically he was still robust looking.

"Mr. Rice," Jack greeted the man, shaking hands.

"Hello, Jack," Rice said. "How's your father?"

"Cranky, like always," Jack said.

"Give him my best, will you?"

"Well, you may be seeing him yourself pretty soon, Mr. Rice," Tyler told the older man.

"Oh? Why is that?"

"Because you're gonna give me a look at his will."

"I am?" the man asked, looking surprised.

"Yes . . . now."

"Jack, you know I can't do that. Your father would—"

"I'm not asking you, Rice, I'm telling you as the sheriff of this town. I'm investigating a shooting, and I need to look at my father's will."

"Who was shot?"

Tyler leaned forward, pushing his jaw out at Rice over the man's desk and said, "I was."

"Well, I'm sorry about that, Jack—"

"Sheriff," Tyler corrected him.

The old man stopped for a moment to take a good look at Jack Tyler's face, and he saw just enough of Zack Tyler there to scare him.

"Sheriff, I'd like to help—"

"You'll show me the will right now, Rice, or I'll put you in a cell for obstructing justice."

Tyler must have done some reading up on the law the night before, Clint thought.

The old man was a lawyer, but he was also an old man, and the thought of spending time in a cell—whether it was legal or not—just did not sit right with him.

"You're putting me in an awkward situation, Ja—uh, Sheriff," Rice said.

"I mean to," Tyler replied.

"You'll have to answer to your father for this," Rice said. "He'll have to be told—"

"And I'm the one who'll tell him," the sheriff finished. "Now stop stalling and get me that will."

"What about these gentlemen?"

"These gentlemen are my duly sworn deputies," Tyler lied. "Now, do you have any other objections?"

"Some," Rice said, "but you wouldn't listen." Rice turned and bent over a small safe behind his desk. Clint could hear the tumblers as the lawyer opened the safe and took out a long, white envelope. He turned to the sheriff, holding the envelope close to his breast.

"I'm giving you a chance to reconsider, Sheriff," he said, but Tyler just stuck out his hand and the lawyer reluctantly gave him the will.

"You're just like your old man, Jack," he said. "Stubborn."

"I don't know if you mean that as a compliment or a criticism, Bob, but I'll take it both ways," Tyler said.

He opened the envelope and took out the document. Clint and Bags stayed where they were and allowed the sheriff to read what his father had declared should happen after his death.

When he was finished Clint expected him to put the document back in the envelope and return it to Rice, but instead he handed it to Bags, who read it and passed it on to Clint. The Gunsmith scanned it, then handed it back to Tyler.

"All right," Tyler said, handing it back to Rice. "Put it away. You can let my father know about this if you want to, but I'm telling you that I'm going out there and I'll tell him myself."

"I believe you," Rice said, putting the envelope away. "Just make sure you tell him that you left me no choice. Just the way he would have done."

"I'll tell him," Tyler said. He turned and walked out, and Clint and Bags followed.

"You both read it," Tyler said. "Does it mean the same thing to you without the legal mumbo jumbo that it does to me?"

"The ranch and all his holdings get split evenly between the three brothers," Clint said. "If any of you die before he does, then everything gets split between the remaining brothers."

"I guess that gives Cliff a pretty good motive to want to

get rid of you," Bags said.

"And what about Ben?" Clint said.

"Yeah, I guess it gives him a motive, too," Jack admitted.

"No, that's not what I meant," Clint said.

"Then what?"

"After Cliff killed you, what would happen to Ben?" Clint asked. "Would Cliff split everything with him, or would he try to kill him, too?"

"I don't know," Jack said. "I think he might want to keep Ben around to do his dirty work. He'd gain control of Ben's half soon enough, anyway."

"Does this mean you accept the idea that your brothers are the ones who tried to kill you last night?"

"I might, except for one thing," Jack said.

"What's that?"

"Cliff is a crack shot, and Ben isn't far behind," Jack explained. "With all of the torches last night, there was plenty of light."

"You're saying that if they wanted to kill you, they would have," Bags said.

"Right."

"In that case whichever one fired the shot—Cliff or Ben—hit you in the arm on purpose," Bags said.

"It's possible."

"There are other possibilities," Clint said.

"Name them," Jack Tyler said.

"Well, you might not like them," Clint said, "but I think we should discuss them before we go rushing out to your father's ranch."

"I'm willing," the sheriff said.

"Then let's go over to your office and talk about it," Clint suggested.

"Let's go," Tyler said, and strode off toward the office.

"What are you thinking about?" Bags asked, hooking

Clint's arm before the Gunsmith could follow the law-man.

"Somebody else with a motive for the shooting," Clint said. "Somebody with everything to gain."

Chapter Forty

"Me?" Jack Tyler said. "Why would I arrange to have myself shot?"

"Sympathy wins a lot of votes," Clint said. "I've seen it used in the past."

"And used it a couple of times yourself, no doubt," Tyler retorted.

"Not this way," Clint said.

"Well I didn't use it this way, either," Tyler said. "You think I had one of my brothers shoot me in the arm from that rooftop? That's a laugh. Neither one of them is on speaking terms with me."

"Still, Cliff would rather see you remain sheriff. That way, he'd hold onto the ranch."

"I don't want the ranch," Tyler said. "All right, I admit that I stretched the truth to you a little bit. I didn't want the sheriff's job at first, but now I do—but I wouldn't kill Bags to get it, and I certainly wouldn't risk my own life."

"You could have gotten someone else to take the shot," Clint suggested.

"The fact of the matter is," Tyler said, "if I did want to pull a stunt like that, Cliff's the one I'd want behind the rifle—but I don't think he'd go along with it."

"He would if Zack told him to," Clint said.

"Maybe," Tyler said. "Tell me, though, what are you

trying to link me to, the shooting last night, or the shot taken at Bags?''

''I'm not trying to link you to anything,'' Clint said. ''I said there were other possibilities, and I'm exploring them.''

''Well, are there any others that don't hinge on me being involved?'' Tyler asked.

''There was another one,'' Clint said, ''but I haven't worked it out in my mind, yet.''

''Is it too much to ask that you let us in on it?'' the sheriff asked. ''After all, we're just the law in this town.''

''One way or another,'' Clint said, ''one of you will still be the law after the election on Thursday.''

''Are you suggesting we put this off until then?'' Bags asked.

''Not really,'' Clint said. ''One of you may also be dead by Thursday.''

''Cheerful thought,'' Bags replied.

''I want to know about this other possibility,'' Tyler said, ''before we leave this office.''

Clint caught Tyler's eyes and held them, and saw the determination there. ''All right.'' He paused. ''Fran.''

''My sister?'' Jack asked in surprise. ''Little Fran?''

''Can she shoot?''

''I don't know.''

''How does she feel about you, your brothers and your father?''

''I don't know, exactly,'' Tyler admitted.

''You don't know very much about Fran, do you?'' Clint asked.

''We never got along very well,'' he said.

''That seems to be a trait that runs in your family,'' Clint observed.

''In a lot of families,'' Jack said, in meager defense of the Tyler clan.

''Bags, did you notice what Fran gets from Zack's will?'' Clint asked.

"Uh, no, not really," Bags admitted. "I was kind of concentrating on the brothers."

"How about you, Jack?" Clint said, calling Tyler by his first name for the first time.

"I don't recall."

"I do," Clint said. "She's not even mentioned in the will. In fact, as far as all of you are concerned, she doesn't exist—except when the old man needs a meal or an errand."

Frowning, Tyler said, "I guess I never thought about her much."

"I guess none of you did," Clint said. "And how do you think she feels about that?"

"I can see why she might want to shoot me," Tyler said, "but what about Bags? Why would she want to kill him?"

"I said these were possibilities," Clint said again. "I didn't say I had all of the answers."

"Well, I say we get all of the answers," Tyler said, standing up. "Let's get this cleared up before the election, so we don't have to be looking over our shoulder at every voter."

Clint looked over at Bags, who shrugged and said, "That's fine with me."

"Well, if you two lawmen don't mind, I'd kind of like to tag along and see the end," Clint said.

"Jesus," Bags said. "I hope it's not *the* end."

Chapter Forty-One

When the three of them approached the front gate of the Big T, a ranch hand hesitated long enough about letting them in for Tyler to get angry about it.

"Open the damned gate, Holman," Tyler ordered in his sternest lawman tone, "before I batter it open with you."

"All right, all right, Mr. Tyler," the man said. "I was just following orders."

"Sheriff Tyler to you," Jack said, "and what orders are those?"

"Not to let either the deputy or Adams through the front gate."

"Well, they're with me, so open the goddamned gate!"

"Yes, sir!" Holman said, because there was something about Jack Tyler right at that moment that reminded him of old man Zack a few years ago.

"Let's go," Tyler said, and rode through.

Clint and Bags exchanged glances, then shrugged and followed.

They rode up to the front of the house and when Tyler dismounted he told the hand there, "Keep all three horses out here."

"Yes, sir."

"Let's go in."

"Lead the way," Clint said.

The sheriff opened the front door and strode in, with Bags and Clint close on his heels.

"Looks like nobody's around," Bags said.

"The old man will be upstairs," Jack said, and he started up the stairs. Bags began to follow, but Clint grabbed his arm.

"Take a look around, Bags," he said. "See if you can locate the rest of the family."

"Right."

Bags went his way, and Clint went up the stairs after the sheriff.

"This way," Tyler said from in front of Zack's room.

"Who's that?" a voice called from the room. "Who's out there, damn it?"

"It's Jack," Tyler called.

"Come on in," Zack invited.

"What are you waiting for?" Clint asked.

"You're making me think twice with all this talk about the family," Jack whispered. "The old man's got a sawed-off under the bed."

With that Jack Tyler drew his gun, and Clint did the same.

"Don't shoot him unless you have to," Tyler said.

"I wouldn't think of it."

"Now!" Tyler said.

They both sprang into the room, Tyler cutting to the left, and Clint to the right, guns trained on the man in the bed.

"What the hell do you think you're doing?" Zack Tyler demanded.

He was empty-handed.

"Under the bed," Jack Tyler said.

Clint moved forward while Jack covered his father, reached under the bed and came away with the sawed-off.

"What the hell is going on, Jack?" the old man demanded further.

"Just pulling your fangs, old man," Jack said, holstering his gun. "Where are the others?"

"What others?"

"Cliff, Ben, and Fran," Jack said.

"Working, I imagine," Zack said. "You had better tell me what the hell is going on here, boy, or I'll—"

"Save the threats," Jack said. "I'm going to do the talking, and you are going to listen."

Zack had an idea of replying, but he saw a look in Jack's eye that kept him silent.

"Somebody tried to kill me last night," Jack told his father, "and I want to know if you had anything to do with it."

"You think I dragged myself out of this bed to take a shot at you?" Zack asked.

"Just answer the question!" Jack Tyler snapped.

"I didn't have anything to do with it," Zack said. "Hell, I threw that barbecue to try and make sure you got the sheriff's job again. Why would I want to kill you?"

"Maybe you didn't," Clint said.

"You're Adams?" the old man asked, squinting at Clint.

"That's right."

"What do you mean, maybe I didn't?"

"Maybe you sent Cliff to shoot Jack in the arm, hoping for some sentimental votes."

Zack looked at Clint silently for a few moments, then grinned—or at least, when his puckered mouth widened, Clint assumed it was supposed to be a grin—and said, "I didn't, but by damn, if I had thought of it, I would have."

Clint looked at Jack and said, "Do you believe him?"

"He's a lot of things," Jack said, "but he's not a liar. Yeah, I believe him."

Clint bent forward and replaced the sawed-off underneath the bed.

"That doesn't rule out Cliff making some kind of a half-ass decision on his own," Zack said. "That boy is out for my job, if you catch my drift."

"He can have it," Jack said, "but not at my expense. Where is he?"

"You gonna take him on?" Zack asked, with interest.

"That's none of your business, old man. You just lay back there on your pillows and wait for us to sort it all out."

Jack walked out of the room, but Clint stayed behind to talk to old Zack.

"There's something different about that boy," Zack said, looking at Clint.

"He probably reminds you of yourself," Clint said.

Zack looked surprised, but then considered the statement and said, "You're right, he does. By God, he sure does." The old man actually looked happy. "You know how long I been waiting for one of my boys to remind me of me?"

"I thought it was generally considered that Cliff thought like you," Clint said.

"He's crafty like me," Zack said, "but he ain't as smart or mean as I was—hell, as I am."

"Somebody took a shot at Deputy Bags after he left you, and then at Jack last night. What do you think?"

"You think it's Cliff?" Zack asked. "What's his motive?"

"We went through that some," Clint said. "We went to see your lawyer and got a look at your will—"

"You what?" Zack roared. "That old toad let you look at my will? By whose authority?"

"Sheriff Jack Tyler," Clint answered.

Again the old man's face registered surprise, but he did not object anymore to the invasion of his will.

"You think Cliff would kill Jack so he could get half of everything instead of a third?"

"There's another consideration."

"Ben?" Zack asked, really surprised now. "Ben's not smart enough."

"Not Ben," Clint said, and did not elaborate. He wanted to see if Zack would come up with Fran's name on his own.

After a moment to think about it, however, all Zack said was, "Who then?"

The girl just simply didn't exist as far as her family was concerned.

"Fran."

"You're crazy!"

"Did you send her to see me some nights ago?"

"I did," he said. "I wanted her to find out whether or not you were helping Joe Bags with his campaign. I gather she stayed the night, but refused to do as I asked?"

"She disappeared the next morning," Clint said. "I haven't seen her since."

"And now you think that she has something to do with these shootings?"

"Maybe she's just looking for attention," Clint suggested, but he didn't think it was all that simple. "You left her out of the will totally. Any special reason for that?"

"Reason?" Zack repeated. "No, there was no special reason. Why, I don't think I even thought about her while I was making it."

"That's why I think she has something to do with this," Clint said. "I don't know what exactly. Can she shoot?"

"I don't know."

"Nobody knows anything about her," Clint said in disbelief. "I've got to find her and talk to her."

"I think you're wasting your time," Zack said.

"I'll let you know," Clint said to the old man. "If you care, that is."

"I care about this ranch," Zack said, "and my name."

"And everything else you own," Clint added. "Like the town."

"Right."

"It's a little late for this advice, Zack," Clint said, the name coming easily because everyone else used it, "but you might have taken some time over the years to worry about your family."

Chapter Forty-Two

When Clint came downstairs he found Jack Tyler peering out the front window.

"What took you so long?"

"I had a talk with your old man," Clint said, "and fulfilled a promise you made to Robert Rice."

"The will," Tyler said.

"I told him," Clint said. "I think for the first time in his life, old Zack is proud of somebody other than himself."

"A little too late," Jack said. "Where'd Bags go?"

"I sent him to try and locate the others," Clint said. "I only hope he didn't end up finding trouble."

"If he found Ben and Cliff together, then he found trouble," Jack said.

"If I can make a suggestion," Clint said, "I think we should split up. You look for Bags and your brothers, and I'll look for Fran."

"I think you're wrong about Fran," Jack said.

"So does Zack," Clint said, "but when somebody is treated all her life like she doesn't exist, something has got to give."

"Go ahead then," Jack said. "Try and prove your point, just be careful. If you look for Fran and run into one of the others, you better be prepared."

"I'll keep that in mind."

173

Both men left the house by way of the front door, and Jack told Clint, "Try off that way."

"What's that way?"

"The barn, the corral, and Fran has a garden there."

"How do you know that?"

Jack looked embarrassed for a moment, then said, "I saw it once."

They split up, Clint moving away on foot while Jack mounted up and rode the other way. Bags's horse was still in front of the house, as was Duke. Before starting his search, Clint walked over to Duke and noticed that the hand who had taken the horses from them had secured Duke's reins to a hitching-rail. Clint loosened the reins, patted the big black on the neck and said, "Wait here, big boy."

Clint passed a couple of cowhands on his way to the barn, but neither man gave him more than a glance. Stopping strangers just wasn't part of their job.

He found Fran's garden on the side of the barn. It was small, but she seemed to have a good variety of vegetables. From the looks of it, however, it had not been tended for the past couple of days.

There were a couple of horses in the corral which, from the look of them, were probably unbroken.

Moving around to the front of the barn he tried the oversized doors and found them unlocked. He swung one of them wide open and looked inside. There was no one in sight so he stepped inside to have a better look around.

Just inside the doors he stopped and looked down at the dirt floor. There were two parallel lines worn into the dirt, the kind a man's bootheels might make if he were being dragged. Clint followed the trail with his eyes and saw that it led behind a stack of baled hay. Drawing his gun, he followed the path made by the two grooves and when he moved around the hay bales, he found the cause.

Ben Tyler was lying on the ground, on his side, with a baling hook stuck in his back. There was some blood around him, and his eyes were wide open and glazed over. He was very dead.

Ben's death was easily reconstructed. As he had stepped into the barn, someone had come up behind him and drove the baling hook into his back. They then dragged him around behind the bales of hay. As long as the hook was still in his back, the blood seeped out slowly, instead of gushing out, as it would have had the hook been removed.

Clint holstered his gun, but as he did he heard a familiar sound from behind him: the audible click of the hammer being thumbed back on a gun.

"Leave the gun in your holster, Clint," a voice said, "and unbuckle your gunbelt."

"Fran—" he started.

"Just do it!" she ordered, and there was a touch of hysteria to her voice. "I know how good you are with your gun, but if you try for it I'll have to kill you."

"All right, Fran," he said, "all right. Just take it easy and I'll do as you say."

Slowly—and reluctantly—he reached down, unbuckled his gunbelt and allowed it to fall to the ground.

"Kick it away," she instructed, and he obeyed.

"Now turn around."

He turned and was startled by what he saw. Fran was standing there holding a Walker Colt that was much too large for her hands. Her clothing was covered with blood, probably from Ben, and her face was smeared with dirt and tears.

"Fran, let me help you."

"I was," she said. "I was going to ask you to help me that night, in your room, but I couldn't. You'd never have helped me if you knew what I was planning to do."

"Kill your brothers?"

"My half brothers!" she almost screamed. "They were never my brothers, they never tried to be my brothers."

"That's a good reason to leave, Fran," Clint said, "but

not to kill them. Why kill them? And why now?''

''Pa's ready to die,'' she said, ''and when he does the boys will get everything.''

Clint frowned and asked, ''You've seen the will?''

She laughed then, although there was no humor in it. ''I don't have to see the will to know that I get nothing,'' she said. ''I know old Zack, I know the way he thinks.''

''But why kill them?'' he asked again.

''This is my home,'' she said. ''I have a garden. Did you see my garden?''

''I saw the garden,'' he said. ''It's very nice.''

''I spend a lot of time on that garden,'' she said. ''When Zack dies, Cliff will be in charge, and he'd send me away. Then who'd take care of my garden?''

''Fran—''

''So they have to die,'' she said. ''All three of them. It would all be mine then, wouldn't it? Because I'd be the only surviving Tyler.''

''Fran, why try to kill Joe Bags?'' he asked.

''That wasn't me,'' she said. ''That was Cliff. He was afraid that if Jack lost the election, he'd come back and take over the ranch. But that gave me the idea.''

''You tried to kill Jack first.''

She nodded. ''I knew about the speech, so I rode into town early, used a key to get into the warehouse and hide. When Jack started his speech I went up to the roof.''

''How come you missed?''

''I'm usually a pretty good shot,'' she said, ''but I couldn't judge well enough with the downward angle, and it was also the first time I had ever shot at a man. I was scared.''

''Where'd you go after the shot?''

She laughed again and said, ''I was in the warehouse while you were stumbling around. I'm small enough to hide in one of the feed boxes. I used to do it when I was little, too.''

''You did that,'' Clint said, pointing back at Ben.

She nodded and said, "Yes. Ben was the easiest, I should have done him first all along. He's not too smart."

"What about Cliff and Jack?" he asked. "How do you intend to get them?"

"I've already killed Cliff," she said, surprising him.

Reflexively he looked around him, but she said, "He's up in the hayloft."

Clint looked up then, wondering how she had gotten Cliff up there.

"Cliff has been looking at me ever since I turned sixteen," she explained to him. "Not as a sister, but as a woman."

"So you lured him into the hayloft—"

"He came very willingly, Clint," she said. "You know how good I am in bed. He never found out."

"How—"

"I put a knife in his back," she said. Looking down at herself she said, "Some of this blood is Ben's, but most of it is Cliff's. He bled a lot."

"So then Jack is the only one left," Clint said.

"After you," she said. "You know now, and I can't let you tell. I think I'm falling in love with you, Clint, but you understand that I can't let you tell. I'd lose my garden for sure, then."

"Fran, I can help you—"

"You say that, but you wouldn't help me kill Jack. You're not like that."

"I don't think you are, either," he said. "Not really."

"Oh, I am," she said, nodding her head, "I definitely am. They made me that way, all of them—Pa especially."

"Are you going to kill Zack too?"

"I couldn't kill Zack, she said, looking at him strangely for suggesting such a thing. "He's my father. I killed them because they *weren't* my brothers. Don't you see?"

All Clint could see at that point was that his life was hanging by a thread unless he could keep her talking until either Bags or Jack Tyler came looking for him.

"So Zack will just die on his own of natural causes, and you'll get everything."

"Right."

"And are people just going to forget the fact that three men were killed out here?"

"It doesn't matter," she said. "They won't suspect me. No one ever thinks of me."

"I did."

"That's why I was falling in love with you."

"No, you don't understand," he said. "I suspected you of having something to do with the shootings."

That stopped her for a few moments. "You did?"

"Yes."

She looked at the gun in her hand and said, "This is Cliff's gun. I'm going to have to use it on you now."

"Fran—" he said, but she extended both of her arms in front of her, holding the heavy gun in both hands.

"Fran!" someone else shouted, and she looked toward it without lowering the gun. Clint looked also.

It was Jack Tyler, standing in the doorway with his gun pointed at his sister—*half* sister.

"Go away, Jack," she said. "I'm not ready for you, yet."

"Put the gun down, Fran," he said. "It's all over. I heard everything."

"Then I'll have to kill you after I kill Clint."

"Don't be foolish. If you kill us you'll have to kill Joe Bags, too. He came in behind you."

"You're lying."

Clint looked past Fran and saw Joe Bags standing behind her with his gun out.

"He's telling the truth, Fran," Clint said. "The deputy is right behind you with his gun out."

"I'll kill him, too," she insisted.

"You can't kill all three of us, Fran," Jack said. "Put the gun down. Don't make me shoot you."

"What do you care?" she asked him. "Go ahead and

shoot me. I'm not putting the gun down. I have to do this.''

"Fran, Cliff and Ben are dead, and this ranch means nothing to me," Jack told her. "You can have it when the old man is gone. You're welcome to it."

"You're lying."

At that point everyone stopped talking, as if they were all waiting for one of the others to say something. Clint stood stock-still under the barrel of Fran's gun, while Jack Tyler and Joe Bags stood with their guns pointed at Fran Tyler, one in front of her and one behind her.

"Fran," the Gunsmith said, finally breaking the silence, "think about it clearly for a moment. Think about what you're doing, what you've done."

She shook her head violently and said, "No, I don't want to think about it. I just want to get it over with."

"I don't want to die, Fran," he told her, "but I also don't want you to die."

As he was speaking he noticed that Joe Bags was inching closer to her. He had to keep her attention diverted.

"If you shoot me, Jack will shoot you," he said. "What will that accomplish? You and I will be dead, Jack and Zack will be alive. Ben and Cliff, you and I, we will have died for nothing."

"No," she said, "No, you're trying to make me think. I don't want to think."

"Fran—"

"You're talking too much," she said, and then suddenly it was as if she realized what he was trying to do. She turned slightly to her right. With her gun still on Clint, she looked over her shoulder and saw what Bags was doing.

"No!" she shouted. Clint saw her thumbs hastily draw the hammer back on the Colt, and he knew Jack was going to shoot.

"No!" he called out to the lawman, but even as he

shouted Jack Tyler pulled the trigger, sending a hot .45 caliber bullet into his half sister's stomach.

Fran staggered under the impact, and both of her fingers yanked reflexively on the trigger of the Colt, firing a round into the ceiling as she fell.

Joe Bags had thrown himself to the ground as the sheriff fired, and now he got up and rushed to the fallen girl, as did Clint.

Jack Tyler stood in the doorway with his hands dangling down by his sides.

"She's dead," Bags said.

"I didn't have any choice," Jack said aloud. "She didn't give me any choice. She was going to shoot you."

"She would have tried," Clint said. He reached down and picked up the Walker Colt, then walked to Jack to show it to him. "Look at the size of this gun. Even if she had pulled the trigger, Jack, I doubt that she would have been able to hit me. The recoil would have thrown her shot way off."

"I didn't know," Jack said, helplessly. "I didn't think, I just acted automatically."

"I know," Clint said. He tucked the Colt into his belt, then went and picked up his own gun.

"Ben's over there," he said, pointing, "and Cliff is up there." He strapped on his gun. "For a little girl that nobody ever thought about, or remembered, she did a hell of a lot of damage."

Chapter Forty-Three

The election results were posted the morning after election day: Jack Tyler won by five votes.

"Not bad," Clint said to Bags as they both read the results.

"Five votes," Bags said, shaking his head. "I thought I had it, Clint."

"I think you did, Bags," Clint said, "up until the last few days."

"What do you mean?"

"A man who would go after his own family, even shoot his own sister, that kind of man will uphold the law no matter who's involved."

"Even Zack Tyler?"

"Yeah," Clint said. "Even Zack Tyler."

They turned away from the posted results and walked together to Clint's rig. He was on his way out of Tylerville, and he couldn't get away fast enough to suit him.

"Heading right out, huh?" Bags asked.

"Yeah. There's no reason for me to stay here anymore. What about you?"

Bags took a hunk of tin out of his pocket and pinned it to his shirt.

"I spoke to the sheriff today, and he wants me to stay on as his deputy."

"That's pretty generous of him."

"It sure is," Bags said, "especially after I told him that I'd run against him next time, too."

"He knows a good man when he sees one," Clint said. "Maybe next time you'll make it."

"Maybe," Bags said as Clint climbed up onto the seat of his rig. "I came awful close, this time."

"Sure," Clint said, picking up the reins, "but remember one thing."

"What?"

"Close only counts in horseshoes and dynamite."